DEATH OF A CITIZEN

Available from **Donald Hamilton** and Titan Books

The Wrecking Crew
The Removers (April 2013)
The Silencers (June 2013)
Murderers' Row (August 2013)
The Ambushers (October 2013)
The Shadowers (December 2013)
The Ravagers (February 2014)

DONALD HAMILTON

A *MATT HELM* NOVEL

DEATH OF A CITIZEN

TITAN BOOKS

Death of a Citizen
Print edition ISBN: 9780857683342
E-book edition ISBN: 9780857686237

Published by Titan Books
A division of Titan Publishing Group Ltd
144 Southwark Street, London SE1 0UP

First edition: February 2013
1 2 3 4 5 6 7 8 9 10

Did you enjoy this book? We love to hear from our readers.
Please email us at readerfeedback@titanemail.com or write to us at
Reader Feedback at the above address.

To receive advance information, news, competitions, and exclusive
offers online, please sign up for the Titan newsletter on our website:
www.titanbooks.com

DEATH OF A CITIZEN

1

I was taking a Martini across the room to my wife, who was still chatting with our host, Amos Darrel, the physicist, when the front door of the house opened and a man came in to join the party. He meant nothing to me— but with him was the girl we'd called Tina during the war.

I hadn't seen her for fifteen years, or thought about her for ten, except once in a great while when that time would come back to me like a hazy and violent dream, and I'd wonder how many of those I'd known and worked with had survived it, and what had happened to them afterwards. I'd also wonder, idly, the way you do, if I'd even recognize the girl, should I meet her again.

After all, that particular job had taken only a week. We'd made our touch right on schedule, earning a commendation from Mac, who wasn't in the habit of passing them around like business cards—but it had been a tough assignment, and Mac knew it. He'd given us a week to rest up in London, afterwards, and we'd spent it together. That made a total of two weeks, fifteen years ago. I hadn't known her previously, and I'd never seen her again, until now. If anyone had asked me to guess, I'd have said she was still over in Europe, or just about anywhere in the world except here in Santa Fe, New Mexico.

Nevertheless, I didn't have a moment of doubt. She was taller and older, better looking and much better dressed, than the fierce, bloodthirsty, shabby little waif I remembered. There was no longer the gauntness of hunger in her face or the brightness of hate in her eyes, and she probably no longer concealed a paratrooper's knife somewhere in her underwear. She looked as if she'd forgotten how to handle a machine pistol; she looked as if she wouldn't recognize a grenade if she saw one. She certainly no longer wore a capsule of poison taped to the nape of her neck, hidden by her hair. I was sure of this, because her hair was quite short now.

But it was Tina, all right—expensive furs, cocktail dress, and hairdo notwithstanding. She looked at me for a moment without expression, across that room of chattering people, and I couldn't tell if she recognized me or not. After all, I'd changed a little, too. There was more meat on my bones and less hair on my head after fifteen years. There were the other changes that must have left visible traces for her to see; the wife and three kids, the four-bedroom house with the studio out back and the mortgage half paid up, the comfortable bank account and the sensible insurance program. There was Beth's shiny Buick station wagon in the driveway outside, and my beatup old Chevy pickup in the garage back home. And on the wall back home were my hunting rifle and shotgun, unfired since the war.

I was an ardent fisherman these days—fish don't bleed much—but at the back of a desk drawer, kept locked so the kids couldn't get at it if they should get into the studio against orders, was a gun this girl would remember, the little worn Colt Woodsman with the short barrel, and it was still loaded. And in my pants was the folding knife of Solingen steel that she'd recognize because she'd been present when I'd taken it from a dead man to replace the knife that he'd broken, dying. I still carried that, and sometimes I'd hold it in my hand—closed, of course—in my pocket as I walked home from a movie with my wife, and I'd walk straight at the groups of tough, dark kids that cluttered up the sidewalks of this old southwestern town at night, and they'd move aside to let us pass.

"Don't look so belligerent, darling," Beth would say. "Anybody'd think you were trying to pick a fight with those Spanish-American boys." She'd laugh and press my arm, knowing that her husband was a quiet literary individual who wouldn't hurt a fly even if he did write stories bursting with violence and dripping with gore. "How do you ever think of these things?" she'd ask, wide-eyed, after reading a particularly gruesome passage about Comanche massacre or Apache torture, generally taken pretty straight from the sourcebooks, but sometimes embellished with some wartime experience of my own, set back a hundred years in time. "I declare, sometimes you frighten me, dear," my wife would say, and laugh, not frightened at all. "Matt is really quite harmless in spite of the dreadful things he put in his books," she'd assure our friends happily. "He just has a morbid imagination, I guess, Why, he used to hunt before the war, before I knew him, but he's even given that up, because he hates to kill anything except on paper…"

I'd stopped in the middle of the room. For a moment, all the cocktail-party sounds had faded completely from my consciousness. I was looking at Tina. There was nothing in the world except the two of us, and I was back in a time when our world had been young and savage and alive, instead of being old and civilized and dead. For a moment it was as if I, myself, had been dead for fifteen years, and somebody had opened the lid of the coffin and let in light and air.

Then I drew a long breath, and the illusion faded. I was a respectable married man once more. I'd just seen a ghost from my bachelor days, and it could make quite an awkward little situation if I didn't handle it right, which meant acting just as naturally as I could, walking right up to the girl and greeting her like a long-lost friend and wartime comrade, and hauling her over to meet Beth before any awkwardness could develop.

I looked for a place to park the Martinis before starting over there. The man with Tina had removed his wide-brimmed hat. He was a big, blond man in a suede leather sport coat and a checked gingham shirt with one of those braided leather strings around the neck that Western males tend to wear instead of ties. But this man was a visitor—his outfit was too new and shiny, and he didn't look comfortable in it.

He reached for Tina's wrap, and as she turned to give it to him her free hand lifted casually and gracefully to brush the short dark hair back from her ear. She wasn't looking at me now, not even facing my way, and the movement was wholly natural; but I hadn't quite forgotten those grim months of training before they sent me out, and I knew the gesture was meant for me. I was seeing again the sign we'd had that meant: *I'll get in touch with you later. Stand by.*

It was a chilling thing. I'd almost broken the basic rule that had been drilled into all of us, never to recognize anybody anywhere. It hadn't occurred to me that we could still be playing by those old rules, that Tina's presence here, after all these peaceful years, could be due to anything but the wildest and most innocent coincidence. But the old stand-by signal meant business. It meant: *Wipe that silly look off your face, Buster, before you louse up the works. You don't know me, you fool.*

It meant that she was working again—perhaps, unlike me, she'd never stopped. It meant that she expected me to help her, after fifteen years.

2

When I reached Amos Darrel, on the other side of the room, he no longer had Beth for company. Instead, he was conversing politely with a young olive-skinned girl with rather long dark hair.

"Your wife deserted me to consult with a matronly female about P.T.A.," Amos reported. "Her refreshment needs have already been supplied, but I think Miss Herrera will take that extra Martini off your hands." He made a gesture of introducing us to each other: "Miss Barbara Herrera, Mr. Matthew Helm." He glanced at me, and asked idly: "Who are those people who just came in, Matt?"

I was passing the extra drink to the girl. My hand was quite steady. I didn't spill a drop. "I haven't any idea," I said.

"Oh, I thought you looked as if you recognized them." Amos sighed. "Some of Fran's friends from New York, I suppose... I couldn't persuade you to sneak back into my study for a game of chess?"

I laughed. "Fran would never forgive me. Besides, you'd have to spot me a queen or a pair of rooks to make a game of it."

"Oh, you're not *that* bad," he said tolerantly.

"I'm not a mathematical genius, either," I said.

He was a plump, balding little man with steel-rimmed glasses, behind which his eyes, at the moment, had a vague look that could have been mistaken for stupidity. Actually, in his own field, Amos was one of the least stupid men in the United States—perhaps in the world. This much I knew. Just precisely what his field was, I couldn't tell you. Even if I knew, I probably wouldn't be allowed to tell you; but I didn't know, and I hadn't the slightest desire to find out. I had enough secrets of my own without worrying about those belonging to Amos Darrel and the Atomic Energy Commission.

All I knew was that the Darrels lived in Santa Fe because Fran Darrel liked it better than Los Alamos, which she considered an artificial little community full of dull scientific people. She much preferred colorful characters like myself, who nibbled at the fringes of art, and Santa Fe is full of them. Amos owned a hot Porsche Carrera coupe in which he commuted daily, summer and winter, the thirty-odd miles up to The Hill, as it's known locally. The souped-up little sports car didn't really go with his appearance or what I knew of his character, but then I don't claim to understand the vagaries of genius, particularly scientific genius.

I did understand him well enough to realize that his

present vague, glazed look didn't indicate stupidity, but simple boredom. Talking to us low-grade morons who don't know an isotope from a differential equation bores most of those big brains stiff.

Now he yawned, making only a token effort to hide it, and said in a resigned voice: "Well, I'd better go over and greet the newcomers. Excuse me."

We watched him move away. The girl beside me laughed ruefully. "Somehow, I don't have the feeling Dr. Darrel found me very entertaining," she murmured.

"It's not your fault," I said. "You're just too big, that's all." She glanced up at me, smiling. "How am I to take that remark?"

"Not personally," I assured her. "What I mean is, Amos isn't really interested in anything much bigger than an atom. Oh, he might stretch a point and settle for a molecule now and then, but it would have to be a small molecule."

She asked innocently, "Oh, are molecules bigger than atoms, Mr. Helm?"

I said, "Molecules are made up of atoms. Now you have the sum total of my information upon that subject, Miss Herrera. Please address any further inquiries to your host."

"Oh," she said, 'I wouldn't dare!"

I saw that Tina and her suede-jacketed escort were starting to work their way around the room through a barrage of introductions, under the inexorable leadership of Fran Darrel, a small, dry, wisp of a woman with a passion for collecting interesting people. It was a pity, I thought, that Fran would never know what a jewel of interest she had in Tina…

I turned my attention back to the girl. She was quite a pretty girl, wearing a lot of Indian silver and one of the squaw dresses, also called fiesta dresses, the construction of which is a local industry. This one was all white, copiously trimmed with silver braid. As usual, it had a very full, pleated skirt supported by enough stiff petticoats to form a traffic hazard in the Darrels' crowded living room.

I asked, "Do you live here in Santa Fe, Miss Herrera?"

"No, I'm just here on a visit." She looked up at me. She had very nice eyes, dark-brown and lustrous, to go with the Spanish name. She said, "Dr. Darrel tells me you're a writer. What name do you write under, Mr. Helm?"

I suppose I should be used to it by now, but I still can't help wondering why they do it and what they expect to gain by it. It must seem to them like a subtle social maneuver, a way of skillfully avoiding the dreadful admission that they never heard of a guy named Helm or read any of his works. The only trouble is, I've never used a pseudonym in my life—my literary life, that is. There was a time when I answered to the code name of Eric, but that's another matter.

"I use my own name," I said, a little stiffly. "Most writers do, Miss Herrera, unless they're pretty damn prolific, or run into publication conflicts of some kind."

"Oh," she said, "I'm sorry."

It occurred to me that I was being pompous, and I grinned. "I write Western stories, mostly," I said. "As a matter of fact, I'm leaving in the morning to get some material for a new one." I glanced at my Martini glass. "Assuming that I'm in condition to drive, that is."

"Where are you going?"

"Down the Pecos Valley first, and then through Texas to San Antonio," I said. "After that I'll head north along one of the old cattle trails to Kansas, taking pictures along the way."

"You're a photographer, too?"

She was a cute kid, but she was overdoing the breathless-admiration routine. After all, it wasn't as if she were talking to Ernest Hemingway.

"Well, I used to be a newspaperman of sorts," I said "On a small paper you learn to do a little bit of everything That was before the war. The fiction came later."

"It sounds perfectly fascinating," the girl said. "But I'm sorry to hear you're leaving. I kind of hoped, if you had a little time… I mean, there's something I wanted to ask you, a favor. When Dr. Darrel told me you were a real live author…" She hesitated, and laughed in an embarrassed way, and I knew exactly what was coming. She said, "Well, I've been trying to write a little myself, and I do so want to talk to someone who…"

Then, providentially, Fran Darrel was upon us, with Tina and her boy friend, and we had to turn to meet them. Fran was dressed pretty much like my companion, except that her blue fiesta dress, her waist, her arms, and her neck were loaded even more heavily with Indian jewelry. Well, she could afford it. She had money of her own, apart from Amos' government salary. She introduced the newcomers and the girl, and it was my turn.

"...and here's somebody I particularly want you to meet, my dear," Fran said to Tina in her high, breathless voice. "One of our local celebrities, Matt Helm. Matt, this is Madeleine Loris, from New York, and her husband... Hell, I've forgotten your first name."

"Frank," the blond man said.

Tina had already put out her hand for me to take. Slender and dark and lovely, she was a real pleasure to look at in her sleeveless black dress, and her little black hat that was mostly a scrap of veil, and her long black gloves. I mean, these regional costumes are all very well, but if a woman can look like that, why should she deck herself out to resemble a Navajo squaw?

She extended her hand with a graciousness that made me want to click my heels, bow low, and raise her fingers to my lips—I remembered a time when I had, very briefly, been forced to impersonate a Prussian nobleman. All kinds of memories were coming back, and I could recall very clearly—although it seemed most improbable now—making love to this fashionable and gracious lady in a ditch in the rain, while uniformed men beat the dripping bushes all around us. I could also remember the week in London... Looking into her face, I saw that she, too, was remembering. Then her little finger moved very slightly in my grasp, in a certain way. It was the recognition signal, the one that asserted authority and demanded obedience.

I'd been expecting that. I looked straight into her eyes and made no answering signal, although I remembered the response perfectly. Her eyes narrowed very slightly, and she took back her hand. I turned to shake hands with Frank Loris, if that was his name, which it almost certainly wasn't.

From his looks, I knew he was going to be a bone-crusher, and he was. At least he tried. When nothing snapped, he, too, tried the little-finger trick. He was a hell of a big man, not quite my height—very few are—but much wider and heavier with the craggy face of the professional muscleman. His nose had been broken many years ago. It could have happened in college football, but somehow I didn't think so.

You get so you can recognize them. There's something tight about the mouth and eyes, something wary in the way they stand and move, something contemptuous and condescending that betrays them to one who knows. Even Tina, bathed and shampooed and perfumed, girdled and nyloned, had it. I could see that now. I'd had it once myself. I'd thought I'd lost it. Now I wasn't so certain.

I looked at the big man, and, oddly enough, we hated each other on sight. I was a happily married man without a thought for any woman but my wife. And he was a professional doing a job—whatever it might be—with an assigned partner. But he would have been briefed before he came here, and he would know that I'd once done a job with the same partner. Whatever his success in extracurricular matters—and from the looks of him he'd be the lad to give it a try—he'd be wondering just how successful I'd been, under similar circumstances, fifteen years ago. And of course, although Tina was nothing to me anymore, I couldn't help wondering just what her duties as Mrs. Loris involved.

So we hated each other cordially as we shook hands and spoke the usual meaningless words, and I let him grind away at my knuckles and signal frantically, giving no sign that I felt a thing, until the handclasp had lasted long enough to satisfy the proprieties and he had to let me go. To hell with him. And to hell with her. And to hell with Mac, who'd sent them here after all these years to disinter the memories I'd thought safely buried. That is, if Mac was still running the show, and I thought he would be. It was impossible to think of the organization in the hands of anyone else, and who'd want the job?

3

The last time I saw Mac, he was sitting behind a desk in a shabby little office in Washington.

"Here's your war record," he said as I came up to the desk. He shoved some papers towards me. "Study it carefully. Here are some additional notes on people and places you're supposed to have known. Memorize and destroy. And here are the ribbons you're entitled to wear, should you ever be called back into uniform."

I looked at them and grinned. "What, no Purple Heart?" I'd just spent three months in various hospitals.

He didn't smile. "Don't take these discharge papers too seriously, Eric. You're out of the Army, to be sure, but don't let it go to your head."

"Meaning what, sir?"

"Meaning that there are going to be a lot of chaps"— like all of us, he'd picked up some British turns of speech overseas—"a lot of chaps impressing a lot of susceptible maidens with what brave, misunderstood fellows they were throughout the war, prevented by security from disclosing their heroic exploits to the world. There are also going to be a lot of hair-raising, revealing, and probably quite lucrative memoirs written." Mac looked up at me, as I stood before him. I had trouble seeing his face clearly, with that bright window behind him, but I could see his eyes. They were gray and cold. "I'm telling you this because your peacetime record shows certain literary tendencies. There'll be no such memoirs from this outfit. What we were, never was. What we did, never happened. Keep that in mind, Captain Helm."

His use of my military title and real name marked the end of a part of my life. I was outside now.

I said, "I had no intention of writing anything of the kind, sir."

"Perhaps not. But you're to be married soon, I understand, to an attractive young lady you met at a local hospital. Congratulations. But remember what you were taught, Captain Helm. You do not confide in anyone, no matter how close to you. You do not even hint, if the question of wartime service is raised, that there are tales you could tell if you were only at liberty to do so. No matter what the stakes, Captain Helm, no matter what the cost to your pride or reputation or family life, no matter how trustworthy the person involved, you reveal nothing, not even that there's something to reveal." He gestured towards the papers on the desk. "Your cover isn't perfect, of course. No cover is. You may be caught in an inconsistency. You may even meet someone with whom you're supposed to have been closely associated during some part of the war, who, never having heard of you, calls you a liar and perhaps worse. We've done all we can to protect you against such a contingency, for our sakes as well as yours, but there's always the chance of a slip. If it happens, you'll stick to your story, no matter how awkward the situation becomes. You'll lie calmly and keep on lying. To everyone, even your wife. Don't tell her that you could explain everything if only you were free to speak. Don't ask her to trust you because things aren't what they seem. Just look her straight in the eye and lie."

"I understand," I said. "May I ask a question?"

"Yes."

"No disrespect intended, sir, but how are you going to enforce all that, now?"

I thought I saw him smile faintly, but that wasn't likely. He wasn't a smiling man. He said, "You've been discharged from the Army, Captain Helm. You've not been discharged from us. How can we give you a discharge, when we don't exist?"

And that was all of it, except that as I started for the door with my papers under my arm he called me back.

I turned snappily. "Yes, sir."

"You're a good man, Eric. One of my best. Good luck."

It was something, from Mac, and it pleased me, but as I went out and, from old habit, walked a couple of blocks away from the place, before taking a cab to where Beth was waiting, I knew that he need have no fear of my confiding in her against orders. I'd have told her the truth if it had been allowed, of course, to be honest with her; but my bride-to-be was a gentle and sensitive New England girl, and I wasn't unhappy to be relieved, by authority, of the necessity of telling her I'd been a good man in that line of business.

4

Now, in the Darrels' living room, I could hear Mac's voice again: *How can we give you a discharge, when we don't exist?* That voice from the past held a mocking note, and the same mockery was in Tina's dark eyes as she allowed herself to be led away, accompanied by the Herrera girl, whom Fran had also taken in tow. I'd forgotten the color of Tina's eyes, not blue, not black. They were the deep violet shade you sometimes see in the evening sky just before the last light dies.

The big man, Loris, gave me a sideways look as he followed the trio of women; it held a warning and a threat. I slipped my hand into my pocket and closed my fingers about the liberated German knife. I grinned at him, to let him know that any time was all right with me. Any time and any place. I might be a peaceful and home-loving citizen these days, a husband and a father. I might be gaining a waistline and losing my hair. I might barely have the strength to punch a typewriter key, but things would have to get a damn sight worse before I trembled at a scowl and a pair of bulging biceps.

Then I realized, startled, that this was just like the old days. We'd always been kind of a lone-wolf outfit, not noted for brotherhood and companionship and esprit de corps. I remembered Mac, once, saying that he made a point of keeping us dispersed as much as possible, to cut down on the casualties. *Break it up,* he'd say wearily, *break it up, you damn overtrained gladiators, save it for the Nazis.* I was falling right back into the old habits, just as if the chip had never left my shoulder. Perhaps it never had.

"What's the matter, darling?" It was Beth's voice, behind me. "You look positively grim. Aren't you having a good time?"

I turned to look at her, and she looked pretty enough to take your breath away. She was what you might describe as a tallish, willowy girl—well, after bearing three children I guess she was entitled to be called a woman, but she looked like a girl. She had light hair and clear blue eyes and a way of smiling at you—at me, anyway—that could make you feel seven feet tall instead of only six feet four. She was wearing the blue silk dress with the little bow on the behind that we'd bought for her in New York on our last trip East. That had been a year ago, but it still made a good-looking outfit, even if she was starting to refer to it as that obsolete old rag—a gambit any husband will recognize.

Even after all this time in the land of blue jeans and

squaw dresses, of bare brown legs and thong sandals, my wife still clung to certain Eastern standards of dress, which was all right with me. I like the impractical, fragile, feminine look of a woman in a skirt and stockings and high heels; and I can see no particular reason for a female to appear publicly in pants unless she's going to ride a horse. I'll even go so far as to say that the side-saddle and riding skirt made an attractive combination, and I regret that they passed before my time.

Please don't think this means I'm prudish and consider it sinful for women to reveal themselves in trousers. Quite the contrary. I object on the grounds that it makes my life very dull. We all respond to different stimuli, and the fact is that I don't respond at all to pants, no matter who they may contain or how tight they may be. If Beth had turned out to be a slacks-and-pajamas girl we might never have got around to populating a four-bedroom house.

"What's the matter, Matt?" she asked again.

I looked in the direction Tina and her gorilla had taken, and I rubbed my fingers and grimaced wryly. "Oh, those strongarm guys just get my goat. The louse almost broke my hand. I don't know what he was trying to prove."

"The girl is rather striking. Who is she?"

"A kid named Herrera," I said easily. "She's writing the Great American Novel, or something, and would like a few pointers."

"No," Beth said, "the older one, the slinky one with the black gloves. You looked quite continental, shaking hands with her; I thought you were going to kiss her fingertips. Had you met her somewhere before?"

I glanced up quickly; and I was back again where I didn't want to be, back where I was watching myself every second to see how I was going over in the part I was playing, back where every word I spoke could be my death warrant. I was no longer working my facial muscles automatically; the manual control center had taken over. I signaled for a grin and it came. I thought it was pretty good. I'd always been a fair poker player as a boy, and I'd learned something about acting later, with my life at stake.

I put my arm around Beth casually. "What's the matter, jealous?" I asked. "Can't I even be polite to a good-looking female… No, I never saw Mrs. Loris before, but I sure wish I had."

Lie, Mac had said, *look her in the eye and lie.* Why should I obey his orders, after all the bloodless years? But the words came smoothly and convincingly, and I squeezed her fondly, and let my hand slide down to give the little bow at her rear an affectionate pat, among all those chattering people. Briefly, I felt the warm tautness of her girdle through the silk of her dress and slip.

"Matt, don't!" she whispered, shocked, stiffening in protest. I saw her throw an embarrassed glance around to see if anyone had noted the impropriety.

She was a funny damn girl. I mean, you'd think that after more than a decade of marriage I could pat my wife on the fanny, among friends, without being made to feel as if I'd committed a serious breach of decency. Well, I'd lived with Beth's inhibitions for a long time, and normally I'd have thought it was just kind of cute and naive of her, and maybe I'd have given her an additional little pinch to tease her and make her blush, and she'd have wound up laughing at her own stuffiness, and everything would have been all right But tonight I didn't have any concentration to spare for her psychological quirks. My own demanded my entire attention.

"Sorry, Duchess," I said stiffly, withdrawing the offending hand. "Didn't mean to get familiar, ma'am… Well, I'm going over for a refill. Can I get you one?"

She shook her head. "I'm still doing fine with this one." She couldn't help glancing at my glass and saying, "Take it easy, darling. Remember, you've got a long drive tomorrow."

"Maybe you'd better call Alcoholics Anonymous," I said, more irritably than I'd intended. As I turned away, I saw Tina watching us from across the room.

For some reason, I found myself remembering the wet woods at Kronheim, and the German officer whose knife was in my pocket, and the way the blade of my own knife had snapped off short as he flung himself convulsively sideways at the thrust. As he opened his mouth to cry out, Tina, a bedraggled fury in her French tart's getup, had grabbed his Schmeisser and smashed it over his head, silencing him but bending the gun to hell and gone…

5

A short, dark individual in an immaculate white jacket was presiding over the refreshment table with the grace, dignity and relaxed assurance of an old family retainer, although I knew he was hired for the occasion as I'd been meeting him at Santa Fe parties for years.

"Vodka?" he was saying. "No, no, I will not do it, señorita! A Martini is a Martini and you are a guest in this house. *Por favor,* do not ask me to serve a guest of the Darrels the fermented squeezings of potato peelings and other garbage!"

Barbara Herrera answered the man laughingly in Spanish, and they tossed it back and forth, and she agreed to settle for another honest, capitalist cocktail instead of switching to the bastard variety from the land of Communism. After he'd filled her glass, I stuck mine out to be replenished from the same shaker. The girl glanced around, smiled, and swung about to face me with a clink of bracelets and a swish of petticoats.

I gestured towards her costume. "Santa Fe is grateful to you for patronizing local industry, Miss Herrera."

She laughed. "Do I look too much like a walking junk shop? I didn't have anything else to do this afternoon, and the stores just fascinated me. I lost my head, I guess."

"Where are you from?" I asked.

"California," she said.

"That's a big state," I said, "and you can keep all of it."

She smiled. "Now, that isn't nice."

"I've spent a few months in Hollywood from time to time," I said. "I couldn't take it. I'm used to breathing air."

She laughed. "Now you're boasting, Mr. Helm. At least we get a little oxygen with our smog. That's more than you can say up here at seven thousand feet. I lay awake all last night gasping for breath."

With her warm dark skin and wide cheekbones, she looked better in her squaw dress than most. I looked down at her, and sighed inwardly, and braced myself to do my duty as an elder statesman of the writing profession.

I said in kindly tones, "You say you've been doing some writing, Miss Herrera?"

Her face lighted up. "Why, yes, and I've been wanting to talk to somebody about… It's at my motel, Mr. Helm. There's a rather pleasant bar next door. I know you're leaving in the morning, but if you and your wife could just stop on your way home and have a drink while I run over and get it… It's just a short story, it wouldn't take you more than a few minutes, and I'd appreciate it so much if you'd just glance through it and tell me…"

New York is full of editors who are paid to read stories. All it takes to get their reaction is the postage. But these kids keep shoving the products of their sweat and imagination under the noses of friends, relatives, neighbors, and anybody they can track down who ever published three lines of lousy verse. I don't get it. Maybe I'm just a hardened cynic, but when I was breaking into the racket I sure as hell didn't waste time and effort showing my work to anybody who didn't have the dough to buy and the presses to print it on—not even my wife. Being an unpublished writer is ridiculous enough; why make it worse by showing the stuff around?

I tried to tell the girl this; I tried to tell her that even if I liked her story, there was nothing I could do about it, and if I didn't like it, what difference did it make? I wasn't the guy who was going to buy it. But she was persistent, and before I got rid of her I'd consumed two more Martinis and promised to drop by and have a look at her little masterpiece in the morning, if I had time. As I was planning to leave before daybreak, I didn't really expect to have time, and she probably knew it; but I wasn't going to spoil my last evening at home reading her manuscript or anybody else's.

She left me at last, heading across the room to say goodbye to her host and hostess. It took me a while to locate Beth in one of the rear sitting rooms of the big, sprawling house. We've got plenty of space in this southwestern country, and few houses, no matter how large, are more than one story high, which is just as well. You wouldn't want to have to climb stairs at our altitude. When I found my wife, she was talking to Tina.

I paused in the doorway to look at them. Two good-looking and well behaved and smartly dressed party guests, holding their drinks like talismans, they were chatting away in the bright manner of women who've just met and already don't like each other very well.

"Yes, he was in Army Public Relations during the war," I heard Beth say as I came forward. "A jeep turned over on him while he was out on assignment, near Paris I think, and injured him quite badly. I was doing U.S.O. in Washington when he came there for treatment. That's how we met. Hello, darling, we're talking about you."

She looked nice, and kind of young and innocent, even in her Fifth Avenue cocktail outfit. I found that I wasn't annoyed with her anymore; and apparently she'd forgiven me, also. Looking at her, I was very glad I'd had the good sense to marry her when I had the chance, but there was a feeling of guilt, too. There always had been, but it was stronger tonight. I'd really had no business marrying anybody.

Tina had turned to smile at me. "I was just asking your wife what you were a celebrity at, Mr. Helm."

Beth laughed. "Don't ask him what name he writes under, Mrs. Loris, or he won't be fit to live with the rest of the evening."

Tina was still smiling, watching me. "So you were in public relations during the war. That must have been quite interesting, but wasn't it a bit risky at times?" Her eyes were laughing at me.

I said, "Those jeeps we ran around in caused more casualties than enemy action, in our branch of service, Mrs. Loris. I still shudder when I see one. Combat fatigue, you know."

"And after the war you just started to write?"

Her eyes did not stop laughing at me. She'd undoubtedly been supplied with my complete dossier when she received her orders. She probably knew more about me than I knew about myself. But it amused her to make me read off my lines in front of my wife.

I said, "Why, I'd done some newspaper work before I went into the service; it had got me interested in southwestern history. After what I saw during the war, even if I never got into combat... Well, I decided that men fighting mud and rain and Nazis couldn't be so very different from men fighting dust and wind and Apaches. Anyway, I went back to my job on the paper and started turning out fiction in my spare time. Beth had a job, too. After a couple of years, my stuff just started to sell, that's all."

Tina said, "I think you're a very lucky man, Mr. Helm, to have such a helpful and understanding wife." She turned her smile on Beth. "Not every struggling author has that advantage."

It was the old behind-every-man-there's-a-woman line that we get all the time, and Beth winked at me as she said something suitably modest in reply, but I didn't find it funny tonight. There was that patronizing arrogance in Tina's voice and bearing that I knew very well: she was the hawk among the chickens, the wolf among the sheep.

Then there was a movement behind me, and Loris appeared, carrying his big hat and Tina's fur wrap.

"Sorry to break this up," he said, "but we're having dinner with some people across town. Ready, dear?"

"Yes," she said, "I'm ready, as soon as I say goodnight to the Darrels."

"Well, do it quick," he said. "We're late now."

He was obviously trying to tell her that something urgent required their attention; and she got the message, all right, but she spent just a moment longer adjusting her furs and giving us a pleasant smile, like any woman who's damn well not going to let herself be hurried by an impatient husband. Then they were going off together, and Beth took my arm.

"I don't like her," Beth said, "but did you pipe the minks?"

"I offered you mink the last time we were flush," I said. "You said you'd rather put the money into a new car."

"I don't like him, either," she said. "I think he hates small children and pulls wings off flies."

Sometimes my wife, for all her naive and girlish looks, can be as bright as anybody. As we walked together towards the front of the house, past little groups of people grimly determined to keep the party going no matter what time it was or who went home, I wondered what had happened to send Tina and her partner rushing off into the night. Well, it wasn't my problem. I hoped I could keep it that way.

6

Fran Darrel kissed me goodnight at the door. Amos kissed Beth. It's an old Spanish custom which Beth detests. Just about the time she outgrew the unpleasant chore of kissing her New England aunts and grandmothers, and could get a little selective in her osculation, she married me and moved to New Mexico, where, she discovered to her horror, it was her social duty to take on all comers.

Amos, to do him justice, was one of the less objectionable male kissers of our acquaintance, satisfied with a token peck on the cheek. I think he made that much of a concession to local custom only because Fran had told him that he might hurt the feelings of some of her friends if he didn't. In all social matters Amos took his cue from Fran, since it didn't mean a thing to him, anyway.

Afterwards, he stood there with his vague, bored look while the women went through their goodbye chatter; and I stood there, and found myself suddenly wishing he'd get the hell back inside and out of the light. A guy of his scientific importance ought to have more sense than to hang around in a lighted doorway below a ridge full of desert cedars that could conceal a regiment of expert riflemen. It was a melodramatic idea, but Tina and Loris had started my mind working in that direction. Not that Mac's people were any threat to Amos, but their presence meant trouble, and once there's trouble around, anybody's apt to find a piece of it coming his way.

"It was sweet of you to come," Fran was saying. "I do wish you wouldn't rush off. Matt, you have a nice trip, hear?"

"The same to you," Beth said.

"Oh, we'll see you again before we leave."

"Well, if you don't, I hope you have a wonderful time. I'm green with envy," Beth said. "Good night."

Then the Darrels were turning away and entering the house together, and nothing whatever had happened to either of them, and we were walking towards Beth's big maroon station wagon where it stood gleaming with approximately four thousand dollars worth of gleam in the darkness.

I asked, "Where are they going?"

"Why, they're going to Washington next week," Beth said. "I thought you knew."

I said, "Hell, Amos was in Washington only two months back."

"I know, but something important has come up at the lab, apparently, and he's got to make a special report. He's taking Fran along, and they're going to visit her family in

Virginia and then have some fun in New York before they come back here."

Beth's voice was wistful. To her, real civilization still ended somewhere well east of the Mississippi. She always had a wonderful time in New York, although the place always gives me claustrophobia. I like towns you can get out of in a hurry.

"Well, we'll try to make New York some time this winter, if things go well," I said. "Meanwhile we'd better settle on a place to eat tonight. If we take our time, maybe Mrs. Garcia will have the kids in bed when we get home."

We had dinner at La Placita, which is a joint on the narrow, winding, dusty street sometimes known as Artists' Row by people who don't know much about art. There were checked tablecloths and live music. Afterwards we got back into Beth's shining twenty-foot chariot. If Beth had married a New York broker and settled in a conventional suburb in her native Connecticut, I'm sure she'd have become an enthusiastic Volkswagen booster. It would have been her protest against the conformity around her. In Santa Fe, where they never heard of the word conformity, and with a screwball author for a husband, she needed the Buick to keep her sense of proportion. It was a symbol of security. She glanced at me quickly as I drove past our street without turning in.

"Give them a little more time to go to sleep," I said. "Don't you ever put gas in this bus?"

"There's plenty," she said, leaning against me sleepily. "Where are we going?"

I shrugged. I didn't know. I just knew I didn't want to go home. I could still see Tina's black-gloved hand gracefully giving me the old stand-by signal. If I went home, I'd be expected to make myself available, somehow—take a walk around the house to find the cat, have a midnight burst of inspiration and dash out to the studio to get it down on paper.

I was supposed to place myself alone so they could reach me, and I didn't want to be alone. I didn't want to be reached.

I took us through the city through the sparse evening traffic and sent the chromeplated beast snarling up the long grade out of town on the road to Taos, sixty miles north. There should have been a release of sorts in turning loose all that horsepower, but all it did was remind me of the big black Mercedes I'd stolen outside Loewenstadt—it was the assignment after I'd kissed Tina goodbye and lost track of her—with a six-cylinder bomb under the hood, a four-speed transmission as smooth as silk, and a suspension as taut and sure as a stalking tiger. When I'd glanced at the speedometer—on a dirt road, yet—the needle was flickering past a hundred and eighty kilometers per hour, which translates to a hundred mph and some change. And I'd thought I was kind of babying the heap along.

It almost scared me to death, but for the rest of that job I was known as Hot Rod, and all driving chores that came up were left to me without argument, although I could get an argument from that bunch of prima donnas on just about any other subject… Well, I never saw any of them again, and some of them hated my guts and I wasn't very fond of theirs, but we moved our sniper into position and made our touch on schedule, so I guess it was a pretty good team while it lasted. Mac didn't believe in letting them last very long. One or two assignments, and then he'd break up the group and shift the men around or send them out to lone-wolf it for a while. Men—even our kind of men—had a perverse habit of getting friendly if they worked together too long; and you couldn't risk jeopardizing an operation because, despite standing orders, some sentimental jerk refused to leave behind another jerk who'd been fool enough to stop a bullet or break a leg.

I remembered solving that little problem the hard way, the one time it came up in a group of mine. After all, nobody's going to hang around in enemy territory to watch over a dead body, no matter how much he liked the guy alive. I'd had to watch my back for the rest of the trip, of course, but I always did that, anyway.

"Matt," Beth said quietly, "Matt, what's the matter?"

I shook my head, and spun the wheel to put us onto the unpaved lane that feeds into the highway at the top of the hill. The big station wagon was no Mercedes. The rear end broke loose as we hit the gravel, and I almost lost the heap completely—power brakes, power steering, and all. For a moment I had Buick all over the road. It gave me something to fight, and I straightened it out savagely; the rear wheels sprayed gravel as they dug in. I took us up on the ridge, with those soft baby-carriage springs hitting bottom on the bumps, and swung in among the pinons and stopped.

Beth gave a little sigh, and reached up to pat her hair back into place.

"Sorry," I said. "Lousy driving. Too many Martinis, I guess. I don't think I hurt the car."

Below us were the lights of Santa Fe, and beyond was the whole dark sweep of the Rio Grande valley; and across the valley were the twinkling lights of Los Alamos, in case you were interested, which, unlike Amos Darrel, I was not. They no longer make so many loud disturbing noises over there, but I'd liked the place better when it was just a pinon forest and a private school for boys. Whatever it was Amos had turned up in his lab, and was rushing to Washington to make his report on, I had a hunch it was something I could have lived quite happily without.

Looking the other way, you could see the shadowy Sangre de Cristo peaks against the dark sky. They'd already had a sprinkle of snow up there this fall; it showed up ghostly in the night.

Beth said softly, "Darling, can't you tell me?"

It had been a mistake to come up here. There was nothing I could tell her; and she didn't belong to the catch-as-catch-can school of marital relations. In my wife's book, there was a time and a place for everything, even love. And the place wasn't the front seat of a car parked a few feet off a busy highway.

I couldn't talk to her, and I wasn't in a mood for anything as mild and frustrating as necking, so there wasn't a damn thing to do but back out of there and head for home.

7

Mrs. Garcia was a plump, pretty woman who lived only a few blocks away, so that, except in bad weather or very late at night, she did not have to be driven home. I paid her, thanked her, saw her to the door, and stood in the doorway watching her walk along the concrete path to the gate in our front wall. Like many Santa Fe residences, ours is fortified against invasions of our privacy by six feet of adobe wall ten inches thick. After she'd gone, closing the gate behind her, it seemed very quiet.

I listened to Mrs. Garcia's receding footsteps and to the sound of a lone car going past outside the wall. There was no sound inside and no movement except for our large gray tomcat—named Tiger by the children despite a total lack of stripes—who made a quick, silent pass at the door, hoping to slip inside unnoticed. I closed the screen in his face, locked the door, and reached for the switch to turn out the yard lights. They could be controlled from the front door, the kitchen, the studio, and the garage, and they had cost a pretty sum to install. Beth could never understand why we'd had to spend the money. She'd never lived in such a way as to consider it a luxury, at night, to be able to hit a single switch and determine, at a glance, that there was no enemy inside the walls.

I let my hand fall from the switch without pressing it. Why should I make life easy for Tina and her friend? When I turned away, Beth was watching me from the arch of the hallway that led back to the children's bedrooms.

After a moment, she said, without mentioning the lights, "All present and accounted for. Where's the cat?" If not exiled at night, the beast will hide under the furniture until we've retired, and then jump in bed with one of the kids. They don't mind in the least, not even the baby, but it seems unsanitary.

"Tiger's all right. He's outside," I said.

She watched me cross the room to her without smiling or speaking. The light was soft on her upturned face. There's something very nice about a pretty woman at the end of a party evening when, you might say, she's well broken in. She no longer looks and smells like a new car just off the salesroom floor. Her nose is maybe just a little shiny now, her hair is no longer too smooth to caress or her lipstick too even to kiss, and her clothes have imperceptibly begun to fit her body instead of fitting some mad flight of the designer's fancy. And in her mind, you can hope, she's begun to feel like a woman again, instead of like a self-conscious work of art.

I pulled her to me abruptly and kissed her hard, trying

to forget Tina, trying not to wonder what Mac wanted with me after all these years. Whatever it was, it wouldn't be nice. It never had been. I heard Beth's breath catch at my roughness; then she laughed and threw her arms around my neck and kissed me back just as hard, playfully wanton, coming against me shamelessly and fitting her mouth to mine with deliberate disregard for whatever lipstick she had left. It was a game we sometimes played, pretending to be real wicked, uninhibited people.

"That's better," she whispered a little breathlessly. "You've been looking like a thunderstorm all evening. Now let me go and… Matt, don't!"

It was a game, and I was supposed to know the moment to take time out and let her escape to the bedroom and make a quick change into a pretty nightie, but I couldn't seem to make myself abide by the ground rules tonight. I heard her gasp with surprise and apprehension as I swung her around and let her down on the nearby sofa, following her down and lying against her. But her lips were soft and unresponsive now. Her breast was remote behind layers of clothing.

"Please, darling," she whispered, turning her face from me, "please, Matt, my dress…"

There are times when a husband can't help remembering that he's a fairly large man and his wife's a relatively small girl and that if he really wants to… I put the thought aside. I mean, hell, you can't go around raping people you love and respect. I got up slowly and took out my handkerchief and scrubbed my mouth. I walked to the front door and stood looking out through the glass at the lighted yard, hearing her rise behind me and go quickly out of the room.

Presently I heard the bathroom door close. I turned and walked into the empty bedroom and started to pull off my tie, but changed my mind. My suitcase was already packed, standing by the foot of my bed. Like most old southwestern houses, ours was built with a complete lack of closet space and we've never quite made up the deficiency; in consequence, such things as camping clothes and equipment have to be stored out in the garage and studio. Part of what I needed had already been loaded in the pickup, the rest was ready and waiting for me. By morning I could be in Texas. Normally, I have a good New Mexican's aversion to that loudmouthed state and all its residents, but at the moment it seemed like a fine place to be.

I carried the suitcase to the kitchen door, deposited it there, and stepped down the hall to look in on the baby. Further down the hall there was Matt, Jr., aged eleven, and Warren, aged nine, but they were getting a little too big to get mushy about at night. But you never quite get used to the sight of your own babies, I guess; they always seem like a cross between a practical joke and a miracle from heaven. Our youngest, Betsy, sound asleep, had wispy blonde baby-hair and a square, pretty little face that was lengthening out now as she got her first teeth. She was not quite two. Her head still looked too big for her body, and her feet looked too small for anything human. I heard a sound behind me as I covered her up, and turned to face Beth.

I said, "Shouldn't she have a sleeper on?" When you've nothing whatever to say to your wife as man to woman, you can always fall back on acting like a parent.

"There aren't any; she wet the last pair," Beth said. "Mrs. Garcia washed it out, but it isn't dry yet."

I said, "I think I'll throw my gear into the truck and take off. I can be halfway to San Antonio by morning."

She hesitated. "Should you? After all those Martinis?"

This wasn't, I suspected, exactly what she wanted to say, but it was what came out.

"I'll take it easy. If I get sleepy, I can always pull off the road and take a nap in back." It wasn't precisely what I wanted to say, either, but we seemed to have lost the knack of accurate communication.

We looked at each other for a moment. She was wearing something filmy and pale blue with a negligee of the same stuff, and she looked like an angel, but the moment was past, and I could work up no real interest in nylon angels, not even when I kissed her lightly on the lips.

"So long," I said. "I'll call you tomorrow night if I can, but don't worry if you don't hear from me. I may be camping out."

"Matt…" she said, and then, quickly, "never mind. Just drive carefully. And send some cards to the boys; they love to get mail from you."

Crossing the rear patio in the glare of the lights, I unlocked and pushed wide the big gates that open into the alley that runs alongside our property. In Santa Fe, you're apt to find alleys anywhere. Before we bought the place, the studio was rented as a separate apartment, and the tenant, who didn't have garage privileges, parked his car in the alley. I carried the suitcase into the garage and threw it into the bed of the pickup, which is covered by a metal canopy with small windows at front and sides and a door facing aft. Upon the door, for all following drivers to see, my oldest son had pasted a sticker reading: DON'T LAUGH, IT'S PAID FOR.

I opened the garage doors, drove out into the alley, closed up the garage, returned to the truck, and backed it in through the big gate and up to the studio door. Leaving the motor running to warm it up thoroughly, I went into the studio, which is an L-shaped building at the rear corner of the lot, with thick adobe walls like the main home. One wing of the L serves me as a kind of sitting and reading room, with a studio couch that becomes a bed in emergencies. Around the corner are my files and typewriter. The little cubicle next to the bathroom, which used to be the apartment kitchen, is now my darkroom.

I changed into jeans, a wool shirt, wool socks, and a pair of the light-colored, low-heeled, pull-on boots with the rough side of the leather showing that are sometimes known locally as fruit-boots, being the preferred footgear of a few gentlemen whose virility is subject to question. The appellation is doubtless unfair to a lot of very masculine engineers, not to mention, I hope, one writer-photographer. Dressed, I hauled my bedroll out to the truck, and then loaded the camera cases, as well as the little tripod for the Leicas and the big tripod for the 5x7 view camera. This last I probably wouldn't use once in three thousand miles, but it sometimes came in handy, and driving alone I had plenty of room.

Having been a newspaper photographer before the war puts me in the pleasant position of being able to work both sides of the street. I planned to use the projected trip first for an illustrated article, after which I'd turn around and put the material into a book of fiction.

I wasn't thinking about much of anything, now, except getting packed and away before something happened to stop me. I looked around to see what I'd forgotten, and went around the corner to my desk and reached for my keys to unlock the drawer that held the short-barreled Colt Woodsman .22. I might be a peaceful citizen now, but the little automatic pistol had been my traveling companion too long to be left behind. Starting to put the key into the lock, I saw that the drawer was already open a quarter of an inch.

I stood looking at it for perhaps a minute. Then I put the keys away and pulled the drawer fully open. There was, of course, no longer any pistol inside.

Standing there, I pivoted slowly, searching the room with my eyes. Nothing else seemed to've changed since I'd left the place that afternoon. The other guns were still undisturbed in their locked wall rack. I took a step to the side so that I could look back into the sitting-and-reading area. This, too, seemed unchanged. There were the usual

sheaves of yellow copy paper cluttering up the furniture:
I'd spent the day kicking around some story ideas I
thought might fit what I expected to see in Texas. There
was a Manila envelope on the arm of my big reading chair.
The place is always lousy with those, too, but it occurred
to me now that I hadn't seen this particular one before.

I walked over and picked it up. It was unlabeled and
unmarked. I pulled out the contents: a stapled-together
manuscript of about twenty-five pages. At the top of the
first painfully neat page was the title and the author's
name: MOUNTAIN FLOWER, by Barbara Herrera.

I laid down the manuscript, and walked over to the
darkroom door, turned on the light, and looked inside. She
wasn't there. I found her in the bathroom. She was sitting
in the tub, which was empty of water but filled instead,
with the voluminous pleated skirt and frothy petticoats of
her white fiesta costume. Her brown eyes, wide open and
oddly dull, stared unblinkingly at the chromium faucet
handles on the tiled wall before her. She was quite dead.

8

In a way, I'll admit, it was kind of a relief. I don't mean to sound callous, but I'd been waiting for something unpleasant to happen ever since Tina gave me the sign in the Darrels' doorway. Now, at least, the game was open and I was getting to look at the cards. It was tough about the girl—still hoping to get me to read her damn little story, she must have slipped in here and interrupted something or somebody she shouldn't have—but I'd had people die I'd known longer and liked better. If she'd wanted to stay healthy, she should have stayed home.

Already I had readjusted. It had happened that quickly. Three hours ago I'd been a peaceful citizen and a happily married man zipping my wife's cocktail dress up the back and giving her a little pat on the rear to let her know I found her attractive and liked being married to her. At that time, the death of a girl—particularly a pretty girl I'd met and talked with—would have been cause for horror and dismay. Now it was just a minor nuisance. She was a white chip in a no-limits game. She was dead, and we'd never had much time for the dead. There were living people around who worried me a lot more.

Mac, I reflected, must really have been playing for high stakes, if they were authorized to knock off any casual innocent who might interfere. When necessary, we'd done it over in Europe, of course, but those had been enemy civilians in wartime. This was peace, and our own people. It seemed a little rough, even for Mac.

I frowned at the dead girl for a moment longer, feeling, in spite of everything, a certain sense of loss. She'd seemed like a nice kid, and there aren't so many good-looking girls around you can afford to waste any.

I sighed and turned away, and went out of the bathroom, crossed the big room to the gun rack on the wall, unlocked it, and took down my old twelve-gauge pump shotgun. It bore the dust of years. I blew it clean, checked the bore for obstructions, unlocked the ammunition drawer below the rack, took out three buckshot shells, and fed them into magazine and chamber. The gun had a muzzle device, one of those adjustable-choke gadgets that let you use the same gun for everything from quail at twenty yards to geese at sixty. I set the thing to maximum dispersion, which was still not wide enough to prevent it from putting the full load of nine buckshot into a man's chest—or a woman's—across the room.

It had been a long time since I'd seen Mac, and his people were still, it appeared, playing for keeps. For all I knew, they considered me an outsider nowadays, in spite of the confidential signals that had been passed. It wasn't exactly a friendly gesture, leaving dead bodies in my bathtub. If I was to have visitors before long, as seemed likely, I thought I'd feel a lot happier celebrating auld lang syne with something lethal in my fists.

I went back into the bathroom, set the shotgun by the door, rolled up my shirt sleeves, and bent over Barbara Herrera. It was time to get rid of some of the finer and more sensitive feelings I'd developed since the war. I wanted to know precisely how she'd died; from the front she showed no marks of violence. I found a swelling at the side of her head, and a bullet-hole in back; her long hair and the back of her white dress were bloodsoaked. It wasn't hard to read the signs. She'd been taken by surprise, knocked out and carried into the bathroom, placed in the tub where the mess could easily be cleaned up later, and shot to death with a small-caliber pistol, the sound of which would have been barely audible through the thick adobe walls.

I thought I knew whose pistol had been used, and my guess was confirmed when I saw a little .22 caliber shell under the lavatory. It almost had to be from my gun; Tina went in for those little European pocket pistols with the calibers expressed in millimeters, and Frank Loris didn't look like a precision marksman to me. If he carried a gun at all, it would be something that would knock you down and walk all over you, like a .375 or .44 Magnum. It looked as if they were setting me up for something very pretty, or at least making quite certain of my cooperation,

I reflected; and then, as I eased the dead girl gently
back to her former position, I felt something between
her shoulders, something hard and businesslike and
unbelievable beneath the stained material of her dress.

Very much surprised, I checked my discovery. The
outline was unmistakable, although I'd only met a rig
like that once before. I didn't bother to pull the bloody
dress down to get at it. I knew by feel what I'd find. It
would be a flat little sheath holding a flat little knife with
a kind of pear-shaped symmetrical blade and maybe a
couple of thin pieces of fiber-board riveted on to form a
crude handle. The point and edges would be honed, but
not very sharp, because you don't make throwing knives
of highly tempered steel unless you want them to shatter
on impact.

It wouldn't be much of a weapon—a quick man
could duck it and a heavy coat would stop it—but it
would be right there when someone pointed a gun at
you and ordered you to raise your hands or, even better,
clasp them at the back of your neck. Slide a hand down
inside the neckline of your dress, under that long, black,
convenient hair, and you were armed again. And there
can be situations when even as little as five inches of not
very sharp steel flickering through the air can make all the
difference in the world.

Well, it hadn't worked this time. I straightened
up slowly and went to the lavatory to wash my hands,
meanwhile allowing my estimate of Barbara Herrera to
undergo considerable revision.

"I apologize, kid," I said, turning. "So you weren't just a white chip, after all?"

I looked at her thoughtfully while I dried my hands. Then I searched her thoroughly. In addition to the knife, she carried a little clip holster above the knee—one reason, I suppose, for the squaw dress with its big skirt. The holster was empty. I looked at the dead, pretty face.

"Sorry, kid," I said. "I could have told you how it would turn out if you'd asked me. You just went up against the wrong people. You were cute and smart, but anybody could tell by looking at you that you didn't have enough tiger in your blood. But you had me fooled, I'll grant you that."

There was a ghost of a knock at the studio door. I picked up the shotgun and went to answer it.

9

She made a slender, trumpet-shaped silhouette in the
doorway, in her narrow, straight black dress that flared
briefly at the hem, as was the current fashion—well, one
of the current fashions. I can't keep up with all of them.
She stepped inside quickly, and reached back a black-
gloved hand to press the door gently closed behind her.
She was still dressed as she had left the Darrels', mink
and all. I took a step backward to leave a strategic amount
of room between us.

Tina looked at my face and at the shotgun in my hands.
It wasn't pointed at her—when I aim a loaded firearm at
someone, I like to pull the trigger—but it wasn't pointed
too far away. Deliberately, she slipped the glossy fur stole
from her shoulder, folded it once, and draped it over her
arm, from which a small black bag already hung by a
golden chain.

"Why didn't you turn off those stupid lights?" she
asked.

I said, "I was hoping you'd find them inconvenient."

She smiled slowly. "But what a way to greet an old friend? We are friends, are we not, *chéri*?"

She'd had no accent at the Darrels', and she wasn't really French, anyway. I'd never learned what she was. We didn't ask that kind of question back in those days.

I said, "I doubt it. We were a lot of things to each other in a very short time, Tina, but I don't think friends was ever one of them."

She smiled again, shrugged her shoulders gracefully, glanced again at the shotgun, and waited for my move. I knew it had better be good. You can stand only so long threatening with a gun someone you don't intend to shoot before the situation becomes ridiculous—the situation, and you, too.

I couldn't afford to become ridiculous. I couldn't afford to be the fat old saddle horse, long retired to pasture, now summoned, almost as a favor, for one last, brisk trot through the woods before the final, merciful trip to the fish-hatchery. I was good for something besides fish-food yet, or at least I hoped I was. I'd run my own shows during the war, almost from the start. Even the one on which I'd met Tina had been mine after I joined her, in the sense that I carried and gave the orders.

Mac or no Mac, if I had to be in this one—and the dead girl in the bathroom didn't leave me much choice—I was going to run it, too. But looking at Tina, I knew it would take doing. She'd come a long way since the rainy afternoon I'd first made contact with her in a bar,

pub, bierstube, or bistro—take your choice according
to nationality—in the little town of Kronheim, which is
French despite its Teutonic-sounding name.

To look at her then, she was just another of the shabby
little female opportunists who were living well as the
mistresses of German officers while their countrymen
starved. I remembered the thin young body in the tight
satin dress, the thin straight legs in black silk stockings,
and the ridiculously high heels. I remembered the big red
mouth, the pale skin, and the thin, strong cheekbones; and
I remembered best the big violet eyes, at first sight as
dead and dull as those with which Barbara Herrera was
now contemplating the bathroom fixtures. I remembered
how those seemingly lifeless eyes had shown me a flash
of something fierce and wild and exciting as they caught
my signal across the dark and smoky room that was filled
with German voices and German laughter, the loud,
overbearing laughter of the conquerors…

That had been fifteen years ago. We'd been a couple
of cunning, savage kids, I only a little older than she.
Now she made an elegant, adult shape against the rough-
plastered wall of my studio. She had more shape and
color, she was older and healthier and more attractive—
and much more experienced and dangerous.

She looked at the shotgun and said, "Well, Eric?"

I made a little gesture of defeat and set the piece
against the wall. Phase one was over. I wondered how it
would have gone if she'd found me unarmed.

She smiled. "Eric, *Liebchen*," she said, "I am glad to

see you." Now the endearments were coming through in German.

"I can't say the same."

She laughed and stepped forward, took my face in her gloved hands, and kissed me on the mouth. She smelled a lot better than she had in Kronheim, or even in London, later, back when soap and hot water had been expensive rarities. What her next move would have been I never found out, because as she stepped back I caught her wrist, and a moment later I'd levered her right arm up between her shoulder blades in a good old-fashioned hammerlock, and I wasn't gentle about it, either.

"All right," I said. "On the floor with it, *querida!*" She wasn't the only one who could make with the languages. "Dump the weasels, kid. *Herunten mit der mink!*"

She tried for me with a thin spike heel, but I was ready for that and the latest in cocktail fashions didn't give her much leg-room. I tightened the lock until she moaned a little through her teeth and bent forward to relieve the strain. It put her right into position, and I brought my knee up smartly, hard enough to rattle her vertebrae, against her smoothly elasticized posterior—another writer, more clever than I, has discovered a relic of Victorian modesty in the fact that, while women nowadays may admit to the ownership of two legs, upon formal occasions, at least, they must still seem to possess only a single buttock.

"I'll break your arm, darling," I said softly. "I'll kick your behind right up between your ears. This is Eric, my little turtledove, and Eric doesn't like dead girls in his bathtub. But he can get used to the idea, and it's a goodsized tub. Now shed the pelts!"

She made no sound of assent, but the fur stole dropped to the floor, not with the slithering sound you'd expect, but with a solid, if muffled, thump. Apparently there was a pocket somewhere in that furrier's masterpiece, and it wasn't empty. This hardly came as a surprise to me.

"Now the purse, kiddo," I said. "But gently, gently. The bones take so long to knit, and casts are so unbecoming."

The little black bag dropped on top of the furs, but even this cushion didn't prevent the impact from being noticeable.

"That's two," I said. "Let's say mine and the Herrera's, for the sake of argument. Now how about putting your personal hardware on display for an old friend?" She shook her head quickly. "Oh, yes, indeed, you've got one somewhere. Say the little Belgian Browning, or one of those pretty toy Berettas they've been advertising..." She shook her head again, and I slid my left hand up her back and hooked my fingers into the high neck of her dress. I put some tension on it, enough to cut off her wind a bit. We heard a stitch pop somewhere. I said, "I've no serious objection to naked women, *chiquita*. Don't make me peel you to look for it."

"All right, damn you!" she gasped. "Stop choking me!" I released the dress, but not her wrist. There was a coy little slit in the front of the garment, through which a hint of white skin was supposed to show intriguingly as she moved. She slipped her free hand inside, brought out a tiny automatic pistol, and dropped it on top of the other stuff on the floor. I swung her away from the pile of armaments and let her go. She wheeled to face me angrily, rubbing her wrist; then she reached back with both hands to massage her bruised bottom; suddenly she was laughing.

"Ah, Eric, Eric," she breathed. "I was so afraid, when I saw you…"

"What were you afraid of?"

"You looked so changed. Slacks, tweed jacket, a pretty little wife. And the well-fed stomach… You should watch out. You will be a human mountain, tall as you are, if you let yourself get fat. And the eyes like a steer in the pen, waiting for the butcher. I said to myself, he will not even know me, this man. But you did. You remembered."

She was feeling of her little veiled hat as she spoke, patting her hair, pulling up her gloves and smoothing her dress; she bent over, turning half away as a woman will when her stockings need attention—then she was pivoting sharply, and there was a shining blade in her hand. I took one step back, brought my hand from my pocket, and flicked open the Solingen knife with a snap of my wrist. It's not necessarily the most efficient way to get that type of cutlery into action when you've both hands free, but it looks impressive.

We faced each other, knives ready. She held hers as if she was about to chip ice for a highball; I remembered that it had been strictly an emergency weapon with her. As for me, as a kid I'd been interested in all kinds of weapons, but particularly in the edged ones. I guess it's the Viking in me. Guns are fine, but I'm an old sword-and-dagger man at heart. Anyway, with my reach, I could have carved her like a Christmas turkey, almost regardless of our relative skills. She didn't have a chance, and she knew it.

I said, "Yes, Tina, I remembered."

She laughed, straightening up. "I was just testing you, my sweet. I had to know if you could still be relied upon."

"A test like that could get your throat cut," I said. "Now put the shiv away and let's stop horsing around." I watched her retract the sliding blade of the parachutist's knife and tuck it into the top of her stocking. "Must be hard on the nylons," I said. "Now tell me all about the kid in the john, with her cute little neck-knife and her trick knee holster."

Tina let her dress fall into place and stood looking at me in a measuring and weighing manner. I'd passed the entrance exam, but I could see that she wasn't quite sure of me yet, after all the years of soft living.

I'd been looked at like that before. I could still remember, very distinctly, the pep talk we'd got from Mac, each one of us new recruits, the first time we actually saw him. At least I suppose the others all got it, too. Each candidate was handled and trained individually up to a point, so that if he didn't make the grade he could be turned back to his former branch of the service without too much interesting information in his head.

So I can't really speak for anyone but myself,

but I remember the shabby little office—like all the subsequent shabby little offices in which I was to make my reports and receive my orders—and the compact, gray-haired man with the cold gray eyes, and the speech he gave while I stood before him at attention. He was in civvies, and he hadn't called for any military courtesies. I didn't know his rank if he had any, but I wasn't taking any chances.

Somehow, I already knew this outfit was for me if they'd have me; and I wasn't too proud to take what advantage I could get from a good stiff back and liberal use of the word "sir." I'd already been in the Army long enough to know that they'd practically give the joint to anybody who could shoot, salute, and say "sir." And anyway, when you're six feet four, even if kind of skinny and bony, the word doesn't sound humble, merely nice and respectful.

"Yes, sir," I said, "I wouldn't mind learning why I've been assigned here, sir, if it's time for me to know."

He said, "You've got a good record, Helm. Handy with weapons. Westerner, aren't you?"

"Yes, sir."

"Hunter?"

"Yes, sir."

"Upland game?"

"Yes, sir."

"Waterfowl?"

"Yes, sir."

"Big game?"

"Yes, sir."

"Deer?"

"Yes, sir."

"Elk?"

"Yes, sir."

"Bear?"

"Yes, sir."

"Dress them out yourself?"

"Yes, sir. When I can't get somebody to help me."

"That's fine," he said. "For this job we need a man who isn't scared of getting his hands bloody."

He was looking at me in that same measuring and weighing manner as he went into his talk. As he explained it, it was merely a matter of degree. I was in the Army anyway. If the enemy attacked my unit, I'd shoot back, wouldn't I? And when the orders came through for us to attack, I'd jump up and do my damnedest to kill some more. I'd be dealing with them in the mass under these conditions; but I was known to be pretty good with a rifle, so in spite of my commission it wasn't beyond the realm of possibility that one day I'd find myself squinting through a telescopic sight, waiting for some individual poor dope to expose himself four or five hundred yards away. But I'd still just be selecting my victims by blind chance. What if I was offered the opportunity to serve my country in a less haphazard way?

Mac paused here, long enough to indicate that I was supposed to say something. I said, "You mean, go over and stalk them in their native habitat, sir?"

10

How he'd ever managed to sell the project to someone in authority, I never found out. It must have taken some doing, since America is a fairly sentimental and moral nation, even in wartime, and since all armies, including ours, have their books of rules—and this was certainly not in the books.

I never discovered where or from whom he got his orders. It was fascinating to try to imagine the scene. I couldn't picture a straight-backed West Point graduate actually putting it into plain English; certainly it was never set down in writing, and you'll find no records of our activities in the archives of the Department of Defense, as I understand that mighty, unified organization is known nowadays.

I used to visualize a conference room with a sentry at the door, very hush, with high-ranking general officers in secret conclave and Mac just sitting there in his gray suit, listening.

"There's the fellow von Schmidt," says General One.

"Ah, yes, von Schmidt, the fighter-group man," says General Two. "Based near St. Marie."

"Clever chap," says General Three. This would be in London or somewhere nearby, and they'd all have picked up something of that insidious clipped British way of speaking. "They say he'd have Goering's job if he'd learned how to bend that stiff Prussian neck. And if his personal habits weren't quite so revolting, not that Goering's are anything to cheer about. But I understand that there isn't a female under thirty within a hundred kilometers of St. Marie with a full complement of limbs and faculties who hasn't been favored with the general's attentions—and they're pretty fancy attentions. He's supposed to have a few wrinkles that Krafft-Ebing overlooked."

Mac would shift position in his chair, ever so slightly. Atrocities always bored him. We didn't, he'd say, go around killing people simply because they were sons of bitches; it would be so hard to know where to draw the line. We were soldiers fighting a war in our way, not avenging angels.

"The hell with his sex life," says General One, who seems to be of Mac's persuasion. "I don't give a damn if he rapes every girl in France. He can have the boys, too, for all I care. Just tell me how to get my bombers past him. We take it on the chin every time we come within range of his fields, even with full fighter escort. Whenever we learn how to counter one set of tactics, he's got a new one waiting for us. The man's a genius, professionally speaking. If we're going to be given targets beyond him, I recommend a full-scale strike at his bases first, to knock him out of the air for a time at least. But I warn you, it's going to come high."

"It would be convenient," says General Two in a dreamy voice, after some discussion of this plan, "if something should happen to General von Schmidt during the attack, or maybe just a little before it. Might save the lives of some of our boys, if he wasn't around to give the last-minute orders; besides keeping him from being back in business within the month."

Nobody looks at Mac. General One moves his mouth as if to get rid of a bad taste. He says, "You're dreaming. Men like that live forever. Anyway, it seems like a sneaky and underhanded thing to wish for. But if he should happen to fall down dead, about four in the morning of April seventeenth would be a good time. Shall we adjourn, gentlemen?"

I don't vouch for the language or the professional terminology. As I say, I never learned how it was really done; and I never was a general or even a West Point graduate; and as far as aviation was concerned, it was all I could do, even during the war, to tell a Spitfire from a Messerschmitt. Planes were just something I climbed into, rode in a while, and then climbed out of after we'd landed on some strange and bumpy field in the dark—or jumped out of with a parachute, which always scared me silly. Given a choice, I always preferred to start a mission with a boat ride. I suppose that is another thing I owe to some ancestral Viking; for a man brought up in the middle of what used to be called the Great American Desert, I turned out to be a pretty good sailor. Unfortunately, a great deal of Europe can't be reached by boat.

The German general's name was actually von Lausche instead of von Schmidt, and he was based near Kronheim instead of St. Marie—if such a place exists—but he was, as I've indicated, a military genius and an 18-carat bastard. He had his quarters—you could spot them by the armed guard in front—only a few doors down the street from the tavern I've already mentioned. I kept a long-range watch over the house after I'd made my contact. It wasn't in the orders, precisely. In fact, I was supposed to show no interest in the place at all, until the time came. I didn't really know what I was watching for, since I'd already received from Tina a full report on von Lausche's habits and the routine of the guards, but it was the first time I'd worked with a woman, let alone a young and attractive girl who'd deliberately placed herself in such a position, and I had a feeling I'd better keep myself handy.

The feeling paid off later in the week. It was a gray evening, and Kronheim was having a little wet, belated snow just to make things more pleasant. There was a stir of movement and Tina came running into sight partially undressed, a small white figure in my night glasses. She stumbled past the guards out into the slush of the street, carrying in her arms what was apparently the cheap dark skirt and jacket she'd worn into the place an hour earlier.

I hurried out and intercepted her as she came around a nearby corner. I don't know where she was going, and I don't think she knew, either. It was strictly against instructions and common sense for me to contact her so openly and so close to our target; and taking her back to my place was sheer criminal folly, endangering the whole mission as well as the French family sheltering me. But I could see that I had an emergency on my hands and it was time to shoot the works.

Luck was with us—luck and the lousy weather. I got her inside unseen, made sure of the lock on the door and the blind on the window, and lit a candle; it was an attic room, not wired for lights. She was still hugging the bundle of clothes to her breasts. Without speaking she swung around to show me her back. The whip had made a mess of her cheap blouse and underwear, and had drawn considerable blood from the skin beneath.

"I'll kill the pig," she whispered. "*I'll kill him!*"

"Yes," I said. "On the seventeenth of the month, two days from now, at four in the morning, you'll kill him."

That was what I was there for, to see that she didn't go off half-cocked—it was her first mission with us—to make sure of the touch, and to get her out alive afterwards, if possible. There might be guards to silence; that was also my job. I was kind of a specialist at silencing guards silently. I never touched her, or even indicated that I might like to, those first half-dozen days. After all, I was in charge and it would have been bad for discipline.

"You mean," she whispered, "you mean, you want

me to go back?" Her eyes were wide and dark, violet-black now, deep and alive as I'd never seen them. "Back to that swine?"

I drew a long breath and said, "Hell, kid, you're supposed to enjoy it."

Slowly the darkness died out of her eyes. She sighed, and touched her dry lips with the tip of her tongue. When she spoke again, her voice had changed, becoming flat and toneless: "But of course, *chéri.* You are quite right, as always. I am being stupid, I love to be whipped by the general. Help me on with the clothes, gently…

Now as she walked past me into the center of my studio, fifteen years later and five thousand miles away from Kronheim, I could see a little hairline mark across the back of her bare arm. It wasn't pronounced enough to be called a scar. I picked up her stole and took my Colt automatic from a concealed pocket in the satin lining and tucked it inside my belt. I took a revolver—presumably Barbara Herrera's—from her purse and found that the girl had packed a real weapon under all those skirts and petticoats: one of the compact, aluminum-framed .38 Specials. I'd read about in the sporting magazines to which I contribute fishing yarns from time to time. It was only a handful, light as a toy; and I was willing to bet that with so little weight to soak up the recoil of a full-charge load, it would kick like a pile-driver. I stuck it into the hip pocket of my jeans.

Then I took Tina's gun and carried it, with the rest of her belongings, to where she stood looking thoughtfully at the open bathroom door as if she hadn't quite decided what should be done with what was inside. I put the purse and pistol into her hands, and laid the furs over her shoulders. I touched the little mark on her arm, and she glanced at me.

"Does it still show?"

"Very little," I said, and she turned to look at me fully, and her eyes were remembering exactly how it had been.

"We killed the pig, didn't we?" she murmured. "We killed him good. And we killed the one who almost caught us as we were getting away, and, hiding in the bushes, waiting, we made love like animals to wipe out for me the memory of that Nazi beast, while they hunted us in the dark and rain. And then the planes came in, those beautiful planes, those beautiful American planes, coming right on the hour, on the minute, coming in with the dawn, filling the sky with thunder and the earth with fire… And now you have a wife and three pretty children and write stories about cowboys and Indians!"

"Yes," I said, "and you seem to be doing your best to break up my happy home. Did you have to shoot the girl?"

"But yes," she said, "of course we had to shoot the girl. Why do you think Mac sent us here, my love, except to shoot her?"

11

It changed things. Somehow, even after learning how well she'd been armed, I'd assumed Barbara Herrera was merely a minor character who'd blundered into the line of fire, so to speak. But if she'd been important enough that Mac had made her the target of a full-scale mission...

Before I could frame a question, somebody knocked on the door. Tina and I looked at each other, startled; then I cast a hasty, appraising glance around the studio, reflecting that Beth must have seen the truck still standing in the yard and my lights on, and come over to help me pack, perhaps with a cup of coffee. The only things I could see that might attract her attention were the shotgun by the door, the pistol in my belt, and, of course, Tina.

"Into the bathroom, quick," I whispered, "and flush the john when you get there. Count ten, then close and lock the door." She nodded, and hurried away, moving on tiptoe so the sound of her heels would not betray her.

I turned towards the front door and called: "Just a minute. I'll be right out."

The john flushed—our timing was good—and I tucked the .22 inside my wool shirt, made sure the .38 was well buried in my hip pocket, and stuck the shotgun back in the rack. The bathroom door was just closing. It occurred to me, rather unpleasantly, that it was my wife I was deceiving with such nice, clock-like precision, and with the aid of another woman, a former mistress, to boot. But there was no alternative. I could hardly explain Tina's presence without going into details I wasn't free to divulge, nor could I very well escort Beth into the bathroom, show her the thing in the tub, and suggest that she grab a shovel from the garage and start digging… Thinking along these lines, I pulled the studio door open, and saw Frank Loris's bulky figure outside.

Even if I didn't like the man, it was a relief. I stepped back to let him in, and closed the door behind him.

"Where is she?" he asked.

I jerked my head towards the bathroom. He started that way, but Tina, having heard his voice, came out before he reached the door.

"What are you doing here?" she demanded.

"Finding out what you're doing here," he said. He glanced at me briefly. "What's the matter, is he balking?" He turned back and looked her up and down, obviously checking on the condition of her dress and hair and lipstick. "Or have you two been renewing old friendships? How the hell long do you expect me to sit waiting at the corner in the dead chick's car, anyway?"

Tina said, "You had your orders."

"I don't have to like them."

"Where's Herrera's car now?"

"Outside in the alley. And the junk's all in Writer-Boy's truck. I threw it in back just now. Suitcase, handbag, hatbox, raincoat, and a bunch of dresses and stuff on hangers. Your problem, honey. The heap's clean, so now I'll take it the hell down to Albuquerque and bury it like you said. With your permission, of course." He bowed in a burlesque way, and then turned and walked up to me, looked at me, and said over his shoulder: "Has this guy been giving you trouble?"

Tina said quickly, "Frank! If you've got everything out of the car, you'd better get it out of the alley before somebody sees it here."

The big man didn't pay her any attention. He was still looking at me, and I was looking at him. It occurred to me that with his square jaw, curly blond hair, and powerful frame, he might have seemed attractive to some women. He had strange eyes. They were kind of golden brown with flecks of a darker color, and they were set wide apart in his head. This is supposed to be a sign of intelligence and reliability, but I've never found it so. The man with the greatest space between the eyes I've ever seen—a Czech with an unpronounceable name—I had to use a club on to keep from betraying our hiding place by cutting loose on a Nazi patrol that had already passed us by. He'd killed once that day, and it had apparently whetted his appetite; he just couldn't stand seeing all those nice, broad, uniformed backs moving out of range of his gun.

"Writer-Boy," Loris said softly, "don't get independent, Writer-Boy. You were big stuff once, she tells me, but the war's over now. You do as you're told, Writer-Boy, and you'll be all right."

Then he hit me. His eyes gave no warning at all—if the man knows his business, they don't. I shouldn't have been watching his eyes, anyway, but I was still full of peacetime trust and goodfellowship. In peacetime, people don't haul off and poke in you in the diaphragm for no reason at all, and they don't crack you across the back of the neck as you double up, or kick you in the side as you hit the floor…

"Just a sample, Writer-Boy. Just do as you're told. You'll be all right."

His voice reached me only dimly. I wasn't interested in his conversation. I was concentrating on making it look good. The blow just below the breastbone, while half-paralyzing, made a good excuse for bringing my hands to my midsection as I lay curled up on the floor, writhing in agony with my best Grade A writhe. One hand got the shirt open and the other got a firm grip on the butt of the Woodsman pistol. I heard him move towards the door. The doorknob rattled. I sat up with the gun in my hand and aimed it carefully at the place where his spine joined his skull. He never even looked around. A darning needle will kill in that spot, let alone a .22 bullet.

I sighed and lowered the pistol, watched the door close behind him, and listened to his footsteps dying away outside. He'd keep. I had enough dead bodies on the premises already. I got up slowly, and glanced at Tina. Her posture was a little peculiar. She'd slipped the glossy, satin-lined mink stole off her shoulders and was holding it, with both hands, as a bullfighter would hold his cape. Obviously she'd been prepared to fling it over my head to blind me, if she thought I was really going to shoot. It occurred to me that she was getting more mileage out of those furs, in more different ways, than the furrier had ever dreamed of.

She shook her head quickly. "*Chéri*, don't look like that. We need him."

"I don't need him," I said. "I plan to do without him, completely, as soon as it can be conveniently arranged. And I don't need you, either, sweetheart. Goodbye."

She looked at me for a moment. Then she shrugged and threw the minks back around her shoulders. "If that is how you want it," she said. "If you are quite sure that is how you want it."

I looked at her narrowly. "Spell it out, Tina."

"I would think carefully, *amigo mio*. I would not let my intelligence be warped by the jealous actions of one big fool." She moved her hand casually towards the bathroom door. "There is still that to consider."

Slowly, I put the .22 back under my belt. "I think," I said, "it's about time you told me what this is all about. Who was Barbara Herrera, what was she up to here in

Santa Fe, and why did Mac order her killed? How does he get away with killing people in peacetime, anyway?" I grimaced. "When you've finished that little chore, you can go on to tell me why she had to be killed in my studio with my gun…" I broke off. Tina was laughing. I said, "What's so damn funny?"

"You are, *Liebchen*," she said, reaching out to pat my cheek. "You wiggle so amusingly, like the fish on the hook."

"Go on," I said, when she paused.

She smiled into my eyes. "But it *is* your studio, my dear, *and* your gun. And you heard Loris, all the dead girl's belongings are now in your truck. And if I walk out and leave you now, it's your baby."

"Go on," I said.

"I'm afraid you don't appreciate me, *chéri*," she said. "It was really very nice of me to come back to help you. I would not have done it for anyone else. Loris knows it; that's what makes him wild with jealousy… Of course, you can make things easier for us, if you cooperate." She laughed at me, softly. "Think, Eric! A writer—an unstable person, of course—reports finding a pretty girl, whom he just met at a cocktail party, with whom he was heard to discuss an assignation after the party… this girl he now claims to have discovered shot to death, oh, much to his surprise, in his private writing place. But who will believe his astonishment and horror? The murder gun is his! Come now, come now, Mr. Helm"—her voice deepened and took on a masculine quality—"we are all men of the world here! Why don't you just admit that you slipped Miss Herrera the studio key and told her to wait for you, you'd be out—to read her manuscript, of course!—as soon as your wife was asleep… That's what they'll say to you," Tina murmured, still smiling, "if you call the police. And what will you say, my dear?"

There was a little silence. She found cigarettes in her purse. I let her light her own. When she looked at me again, the smile was gone; and when she spoke, her voice was low and intense.

"What will you say, Eric? The war is a long time ago. How long does it take to forget? Thirty years, twenty, or perhaps only fifteen or twelve? There was never any oath of silence, was there; never any stupid oath of loyalty? Mac always said that the person who needed to swear an oath was the person who would break that oath. We fought together at Kronheim, Eric. We loved together. Will you give me to the police now?"

She waited. I didn't speak; it was her show. She drew on her cigarette and blew out the smoke in that proud, surprised way that almost all women use, that looks as if they're forever congratulating themselves on not strangling on the stuff.

She looked at me, and murmured: "I take back the threats, my dear, and apologize for them. For you, there are no threats. I will tell you: I killed this girl, I, Madeleine Loris, Tina, killed her. Under orders, I killed her, because she deserved to die, because her death was thought necessary to prevent another death, perhaps more than one—but I killed her. We guessed, after she talked to you so long, that she might come here to wait for you; we got here first. It was a gamble, and we won. Loris was waiting behind the door. It is the one thing he knows, and he does it well. But she was still alive when he carried her in there. It was I who found your pistol—the only locked drawer in the place, chéri, and what a pitiful little lock!— and it was I who shot her to death, as she had shot others. Do you think she carried a knife and gun for adornment? Do you think we are the only ones who know how to kill?" Tina drew herself up. "But call your police and I will tell them, I will confess my crime. I will not make you pay for it. And I will go to the electric chair, and I will not talk, because I do not need an oath of silence to keep my lips forever sealed. But I will remember that you, who send me to my death now, were once the only man I ever worked with, whom I wanted to… to play with, afterwards. But I will not hate you. I will only remember that beautiful week in London, so long ago…" Her voice stopped. She drew on her cigarette again, and smiled at me pleasantly. "I'm pretty good, don't you think, baby? I should be in the movies."

I drew a deep breath. "You should be anywhere but in my studio, damn you. Where's a rag so I can mop my eyes, and what do you want me to do?"

I mean, no matter what heart-throbs she'd put into it, what she'd said was quite true. I couldn't very well give her to the police, and I couldn't talk. It didn't leave me much choice.

12

Ten minutes later, we had the pickup ready to roll. You could look inside the rear canopy and not see a thing except camera equipment, luggage, and camping gear.

Unless you knew too much already, you wouldn't be likely to look close enough to discover that the luggage wasn't all mine.

I found myself crouching to peer underneath, I suppose to check that no blood was dripping out of the truck bed, no dead white hand dangling, no long dark hair. The years of peace had drawn the hard temper of my nervous system, and I guess you take corpses more seriously in peacetime, anyway. Hell, you've got to. During the war, in enemy territory, caught with the goods, there was always a possibility that you could shoot your way clear; but I couldn't quite see myself whipping out a gun and burning down a bunch of worthy local cops named Martinez or O'Brien.

I helped Tina to join her silent traveling companion

inside. She had to hitch her cocktail dress hip-high to make the tailgate; I heard her swear feelingly in a language I did not understand.

"What's the matter?" I whispered.

"It's nothing, *chéri*. Just a run in one of my best nylons, that's all."

"The hell," I said, "with your best nylons."

I raised the gate, hooked the retaining chains in place, and brought down the canopy door, which opens upwards like a station wagon transom. Before closing it, I stuck my head inside.

"Get over on that mattress and hang on," I said. "And you'd better stick your false teeth in your purse so you don't swallow them. They forgot to supply springs with this thing."

I closed the door, and started to turn away. Then a screen door slammed at the house, and I saw Beth come out of the kitchen and start across the flagstone patio in the glare of the lights. Well, she could have come at a worse time. I locked the truck canopy and went to meet her.

"I brought you some coffee," she said as we stopped, facing each other.

I took the cup and drank from it. The coffee was hot and strong and black, obviously designed to jolt me sober and keep me awake on the road. The coat she'd thrown over her shoulder and the sturdy moccasin shoes into which she'd stuck her bare feet made her blue angel-robes look flimsy and inadequate. There's supposed to be something very sexy about a woman running around outdoors in her nightie—magazines catering to the male taste seem to be full of these elfin creatures—but it just looks kind of drafty and ridiculous to me. Her face looked sleepy and sweet in the floodlights.

"I took time to duck into the darkroom and load up some film holders for the big 5x7," I said, lying unnecessarily, like any dumb criminal. "I hate to do it in a changing bag when I don't have to. Why aren't you asleep?"

"I heard the motor running," she said, indicating the truck, still idling noisily. "I thought you'd already left, and I was lying there wondering what it was. Then somebody parked in the alley for a while, probably just some kids necking, but I… I get a little nervous when I'm alone in the house. By the time they drove off I was wide awake. Be sure to lock the gate behind you, or they'll be using our compound for a lover's lane next."

"Yes," I said. "Well, thanks for the coffee. I'll try to phone from San Antone—as we Tejanos call it."

We stood looking at each other.

"Well, be careful," she said. "Don't drive too fast."

"In this relic?" I said. "It would be a miracle. Well, you'd better get back inside before you catch cold."

I was supposed to kiss her, of course, but I couldn't do it. The masquerade was over. I was no longer M. Helm, Esq., author, photographer, husband, father. I was a guy named Eric with a knife and two pistols, intentions unreliable, destination unknown. I had no right to touch her. It would have been like making a pass at another man's wife.

After a moment, she turned and walked away. I

climbed up into the cab of the truck and drove it out into the alley. I climbed down again and closed and padlocked the big gates. As I walked back to the pickup, the yard lights went out behind me. Beth never could stand to see a light burn unnecessarily...

The truck is a 1951 Chevy half-ton job, with a four-speed gearbox and a six-cylinder engine developing a little less than ninety horsepower, and it'll shove any of your three-hundred-horsepower passenger cars right off the road, backwards, from a standing start. It has no damn fins over the tail-lights, or sheet metal eyebrows over the headlights, and it was built in that happy postwar era when they didn't have to sell cars, all they had to do was make them and call up the next guy on the list. There wasn't any sense fooling with pretty colors under those conditions, and all Chevy's commercial vehicles came through in the same shade of green, which, as far as I'm concerned, is as good a color as any, and a lot better than some of the emetic combinations adorning Detroit's latest rainbows on wheels.

It's a real vehicle, and you can do anything with it. I've hauled a thirty-five-foot house trailer, climbed Wolf Creek Pass in a blizzard, and dragged a Cadillac out of a ditch with it. Anything, as long as you're not in a hurry and don't mind getting half beat to death in the process. Beth claims riding in it gives her a headache, but I don't see why it should: it isn't her head that takes the punishment. She can't understand why I cling to it, instead of trading it in on something newer and faster and more respectable. I tell her that her Buick takes care of our respectability, and I don't want to go any faster. It's almost the truth.

The fact is that before the war, as kids will, I used to play around with some fairly rapid machinery. I raced some and covered other races with my camera; and during the war, as I've already mentioned, I had occasion to do a little driving under fairly hectic conditions. Afterwards, happily married, I said to hell with it. I wasn't going to be that kind of guy anymore. It was like hunting. I wasn't going to tease myself by sneaking out to murder a harmless little deer once a year, after spending four years stalking game that could shoot back. And I wasn't going to tempt myself by putting something low and sleek and powerful in the garage, and then using it to commute to the grocery at a legal twenty-five miles per hour. I was going to give the beast inside nothing to feed on. Maybe I could starve it to death. Down, Rover, down!

Well, it worked up to a point, but some time during the evening I had passed that point, and now, picking my way sedately out of Santa Fe in the dark, I no longer found any satisfaction in the practical aspects of the strong and solid and durable old vehicle beneath me. I could no longer kid myself that I really enjoyed having a truck as my private transportation, not even as a kind of one-man protest against the bloated and over-decorated machines driven by everybody else.

All I could think of was the fact that we sure as hell weren't going to run away from anybody, no matter what happened. Oh, I've worked her over a bit from time to time, when I've felt like getting my hands greasy. She'll still hold sixty-five all day and do eighty in a pinch, but it had damn well better be a long, smooth, straight stretch of road when you wind her out, and you'd better get off the go-pedal in plenty of time before the next curve, or you'll never make it. They build trucks to haul pay-loads, not to run the Grand Prix of Monaco.

Any family sedan built within the past five years could catch us, even those underprivileged heaps with just one exhaust pipe, one measly little single-barrel carburetor, and poor-man's gas in the tank. A souped-up police car would be knocking on the tailgate before its automatic transmission kicked into high. We were practically a standing target, should anybody want us for anything. I'd had the same naked feeling in those damn little planes they'd sometimes used to ferry us across the Channel, the ones that had to move aside for any southbound flock of geese in a hurry.

I just wasn't hardened to it any more, and I drove very slowly and carefully, keeping an eye on the outside rearview mirror; and when Tina rapped sharply on the glass behind me, I almost lost my dinner.

The front window of the canopy matches up with the rear window of the pickup's cab, but neither of them open, so you can't say there's any real communication. I drew a long breath, turned on the dome light, and glanced around. Her face showed up white and ghostly through the two panes of glass. She had her little pistol in her hand. With it, she beat again on the glass, and gestured vigorously towards the side of the road.

I pulled over, jumped out, hurried to the rear of the truck, and unlocked and opened the door.

"What's the matter?"

"Get it out of here!" Her voice, out of the darkness, was harsh and breathless. "Get it out, or I will shoot it!"

I had a wild gruesome thought that she was talking about the girl she'd already killed once. I had visions of Barbara Herrera rising up with blind eyes and clotted hair... Then there was a silent movement in the opening, and our gray tomcat stood there, its green eyes slitted against the street lights and its fur on end: apparently it didn't approve of its company, either. It meowed at me softly. I picked it up and tucked it under my arm.

"Hell," I said, "it's just the cat. He must have jumped aboard while we were loading up. He likes to drive. Hi, Tiger."

Tina said from the darkness, in a choked voice: "How would you like to be locked up with a dead person and have *that*... I can't stand them, anyway. They give me the creepies, the sneaky things!"

I said, "Well, we sure don't want to give you the creeps, do we, Tiger? Come on, boy, let's get you home."

I scratched the beast's ears. It's not my favorite animal by a long shot—we'd only got it because the kids needed a pet and dogs are too noisy for a writer to have around—but in Tiger's book I was a cat man from away back. We were soul-mates, and to prove it he was now purring away like an amorous teakettle.

Tina had made her way to the rear of the truck, with some difficulty, since there wasn't room for her to stand up under the canopy and she wasn't exactly dressed for making progress on hands and knees.

"What are you going to do with it?" she demanded.

"I'm going to take him home," I said, "unless you think we should keep him with us for company."

"Go back? But that is crazy! Can't you just—"

"What? Turn him out here, five miles from the house? Hell, the poor damn fool can't even find his bowl of milk in the morning if you happen to move it across the room. Anyway, he'd get himself run over sure, and the children would miss him."

She said sharply, "You are being sentimental and stupid. I absolutely forbid—"

I grinned at her. "You do that, honey," I said, letting the hinged door drop. She must have pulled back in time; I didn't hear it hit anything on its way down. I set the latch, got into the cab, waited for a lone car to go by, and swung back towards town.

Suddenly I was feeling fine. You can stay tense only so long. I was over the hump. I was driving ten miles out of the way, with a corpse in the bed of the truck, just to take a worthless alleycat home. It was exactly the kind of screwball thing I needed to wake me up out of my panic-stricken trance. I reached out and scratched Tiger's stomach, driving one-handed, and the ridiculous beast rolled over on its back in abject appreciation, all four paws in the air. Apparently he'd never heard that, unlike dogs, cats are reserved and dignified animals.

I tossed him out at the corner, half a block from the house. All the driving around hadn't been wasted. The solution to our problem had come to me, and I threw the truck into gear again and headed out of town by a different route, no longer creeping along and paying no more attention to the rearview mirror than I normally do. If anybody wanted us, they'd catch us. There wasn't any sense in worrying about something that couldn't possibly be avoided.

13

I dropped into low gear for the last steep grade to the mine. Even that didn't quite do it, and I double-clutched into compound low, which is an unsynchronized gear and quite a trick to get into smoothly while the wheels are turning. I hit it right for a change, the lever went home without a murmur, and we ground on up the mountainside in the dark with that fine roar of powerful machinery doing the job it was designed for. It always gives me a kick to throw her into that housemoving gear and feel her buckle down and go to work, using everything that's under the hood, while the big mud-and-snow tires dig for traction...

Maybe that was my trouble, I reflected. I just hadn't been using everything that was under the hood for a hell of a long time.

I pulled up just below the mine entrance, where enough of a level spot remained—most of the road and other construction had washed out or blown away since the workings were abandoned. God knows how long ago—to let me park on a reasonably even keel just short of a small arroyo some rainstorm had cut across the little flat. Beyond this gully, the headlights showed me the barren hillside and the mine opening, a black hole surrounded by weathered, crumbling timbers. It gave me the creepies, as Tina would have said, to think of going in there at night, although why it should be worse at night, I really couldn't tell you. Fifty feet inside the entrance, the time of day—or the time of year, for that matter—would make no difference at all. It was a good place for what we had to leave there.

I cut the lights, got the flash from the glove compartment, and went back to open up the rear end. I heard her move inside; she made her way out onto the tailgate, but when she tried to swing her legs over the edge, something caught and ripped, and she had to pause to disentangle her sharp heel from the hem of her dress. Then I helped her down, and she pulled back and hit me alongside the jaw, with the flat of her gloved hand, just as hard as she was able. She might be fifteen years older than when I'd last known her, but her muscles showed no signs of advanced senility.

"You think it's a joke!" she gasped. "You sit up there on the soft seat with springs and hit all the bumps and laugh and laugh! I will teach you—" She drew back her hand again.

I stepped back out of range and said hastily, "I'm sorry, Tina. If I'd thought, I'd have brought you up front as soon as we were out of town."

She glared at me for a moment. Then she reached up and yanked off her little veiled hat, which had drifted into the neighborhood of her left ear since I'd last seen it, and threw it into the truck.

"You are a liar!" she said. "I know what you think! You say to yourself, this Tina, she is too big in the head after all these years. I will put her in her place, I will show her who is boss, she with her lady-like airs and furs and fine clothes, I will teach her to let her man knock me down, I will teach her to frame me, I will shake her like a cocktail, I will scramble her like an egg!" She drew a long and ragged breath, removed and folded her furs carefully, and laid them inside the truck canopy, out of harm's way. She went through the feminine routine of settling her girdle and tugging down her dress. I heard her laugh softly in the darkness. "Well, I do not blame you. Where are we?"

I rubbed my jaw. It wasn't true that I'd gone out of my way to make the ride rough for her, but I will admit that the thought of her bouncing around in back hadn't brought tears to my eyes, either. With a person like Tina, you take any little advantage you can get.

I said, "If I told you we were in the Ortiz Mountains, or the Cerrillos Hills, would you know any more than you did before? We're back in the boondocks, about twenty-five miles southeast of Santa Fe."

"But what is this place?"

"It's an old mine," I said. "The tunnel goes straight back into the rock, I don't know how far. I came across it doing research for an article a couple of years back. The first gold rush on the North American continent was staged in this part of New Mexico, and people have been prospecting these dry hills ever since. I made a series of pictures of all the old holes I could find. There are hundreds of them. This one's pretty tough to reach; I doubt if anybody gets over here once in five years. I wasn't sure I could make it all the way in without a jeep, but the weather's been dry and I thought it was worth a try."

"Yes," she said. She looked around at the saw-tooth silhouettes of the surrounding mountains against the midnight sky full of stars, and shivered. She pulled up her long gloves to cover her bare arms, hugging herself against the cold. "Well, we had better get to work."

"Yes," I said. "That was one nice thing about the war. You could leave them where they fell."

It took us two trips to get everything out of the truck that did not belong there. Driving away, we did not speak for several miles. Presently she turned the rearview mirror towards her and started combing the dust and cobwebs out of her hair by the glow of the dashboard. I heard a small sound and glanced at her. She was laughing.

"What's funny now?" I asked.

"Mac *said* you'd know what to do."

I didn't really think it was very funny. "I appreciate his confidence in me. When did he say this?"

"We hadn't expected to make the touch so easily or so soon. I telephoned him long distance for instructions. That is why I was not waiting for you in the studio when you came. Also, I had to wear her coat and drive her car to her motel to pack her things."

"What else did Mac say?"

She smiled at me. "He said that, having lived here so long, you should know where to dig a nice deep grave."

I said, "Mac should try digging graves in this country some time. That adobe clay is like rock, which is why I settled for a ready-made hole. How deep a grave did he want?"

"Two weeks deep," Tina said. "Maybe three weeks, but certainly two."

"What happens then?"

"Everything is explained, very quietly, to the satisfaction of the police."

"This I want to see. How do you go about explaining dead bodies in peacetime?"

She laughed. "You think this is peace, my darling? What a beautiful and quiet life you people must lead out here in the West—with gauze over your eyes and cotton in your ears!" She took the purse from her lap, groped inside, brought out a small card, and held it out to me. "We found this among the Herrera's belongings. It only confirmed what we already knew, but I saved it to show to you. Stop the car, *chéri*. It is time we talked."

14

The card identified a female person by the code name of Dolores, with thumbprint and physical description, and stated that she was to be given any assistance she might require in the pursuit of her assigned mission. The card didn't state what that mission might have been. I gave it back.

"So?"

Tina looked surprised. "That's right," she said. "I forget, you have not fought this enemy. They were our noble friends and allies in those days. Well, this is the standard membership card for the action groups, as opposed to the groups of intellectuals who sit around and drink tea and talk about Marx and feel terribly wicked... No, not standard. I take that back. This is a very special card for a very special group. There are very few members of this group, *Liebchen*. Almost as few as there were of us. And the qualifications are the same." She glanced at me. "Do you understand what I mean?"

I had a little of the feeling that, I suppose, a Martian might have upon unexpectedly bumping into a nice, green, goggle-eyed fellow-Martian in the lobby of the Algonquin Hotel in New York, or the Hollywood Knickerbocker.

"That kid?" I said. "Hell, she looked as if she wouldn't hurt a fly. I thought I could spot anyone in our line of work across a four-lane boulevard on a dark night."

"For a child who would not hurt a fly, she was well provided with fly-swatters, was she not? You are soft," Tina murmured, "your senses have gone to sleep. And she was good, one of their best. We expected a great deal of trouble, Loris and I. And as for her age, my sweet, how old was I when we met?"

It was starting to make sense. I should have known that Mac wouldn't have authorized the death of anyone whose removal wasn't dictated by high strategic necessity, whatever that might mean in peacetime.

"We're not avenging angels," I'd heard him say once in London, "and we're not judges of right and wrong. It would satisfy my soul to sign the death warrant of every concentration camp official in the Third Reich, for instance, but it wouldn't contribute much towards winning the war. We're not in business to satisfy my soul or anybody else's. Keep that in mind."

There was, of course, one exception to this rule. Whether to satisfy our souls or prosecute the war, we did try for Hitler himself—that is, certain optimists and egotists among us did, on three different occasions. I had no part in that. It was on a voluntary basis, and I'd taken a look at the preliminary reports on the job and come to the conclusion that it couldn't be done, at least not by me. I wasn't going to get myself killed volunteering for the impossible, although under orders I'll stick my neck out as far as anybody.

After the third attempt—from which, like the first two, no one returned—counter-intelligence started hearing of queries from the continent, reaching the German espionage apparatus in Britain, concerning the possible existence of an Allied *Mordgruppe* aimed at *Der Fuehrer*. This, of course, although a little off the beam, wouldn't do at all. For the Germans to suspect the existence of anything remotely resembling our organization—whether aimed at Hitler or anybody else—was bad enough; what really worried Mac, however, was the possibility of the rumor getting back to the States.

All the Germans could do, aside from taking a few precautions, was squawk; but the outraged moralists back home could put us out of business in short order. Killing Nazis was very commendable, to be sure, but it must be done, they'd cry, according to the rules of civilized warfare: this *Mordgruppe* sort of thing was dreadful, besides being very bad propaganda for our side. I wonder just how many good men and good ideas were sacrificed before the little shiny, cellophane-wrapped god of propaganda. There were times when I got the distinct feeling that even winning the damn war was frowned upon because it might have an adverse effect upon our public relations somewhere, perhaps in Germany or Japan.

Anyway, our activities were sharply curtailed for several months, and all further volunteers for the Big One, as we called it, were told to relax and forget it; henceforth we'd confine our attentions to less conspicuous targets.

Tina was speaking: "Do you think Mac is the only one ever to think of such a scheme, Eric? They have their specialists in death, also, and Herrera was one of them. And she was working very hard. But now she will disappear. She has checked out of her motel. Her clothes and possessions will disappear. Her car will stand unrecognized on an Albuquerque used-car lot with new paint and new identifying numbers, eventually to be sold to some honest citizen. And I, too, will disappear. But I will disappear without my car, with nothing but the clothes on my back and the purse in my hand. My husband will look for me at the hotel; he will be very upset when he does not find me—perhaps even upset enough to notify the police. Maybe it will be announced in the newspapers shortly that I have been found dead somewhere, the victim of a bullet from a certain type of .38 Special revolver, or the blade of a certain type of knife. And Herrera's people, Eric, what will they think? What would you think, in their place?"

"That you'd tangled with the kid and come off second best. That's assuming they don't know you very well."

She. laughed. "It is sweet of you to flatter me. But we hope you are right. They probably already know who I am, who Loris is. If they don't, they will be permitted to find out. They will assume that Herrera met me in the line of business and was forced to dispose of me. They will guess that she went into hiding to see if there would be trouble or if it was safe for her to proceed with her job. They will wait to hear from her, for a reasonable period, at least. Meanwhile, we have gained time. In a week, Amos Darrel will have his report ready and delivered in Washington. He will have adequate protection there."

"Amos?" I said. I wasn't as surprised as I might have been. Instinct had already warned me, I recalled, that Amos might be in danger.

"Who else? Are *you* important enough to be selected for removal, my dear? It may be true that the pen is mightier than the sword, but these people are not known for their devotion to literature. I doubt that they would risk a good operative on you, not even to keep you from perpetrating another book like—what was it?—*The Sheriff of Hangman's Gulch.*"

I said quickly "I never wrote—"

She shrugged her shoulders prettily. "You can't expect me to recall the exact title, *chéri.*"

I grinned. "Okay, okay. But I didn't realize Amos was quite that important."

"He is important enough. Who are the generals of today, where are the battles being fought, Eric? Oh, people like Loris and I and Herrera, we have our little skirmishes, but the real front lines are located in the laboratories, are they not? And if a key man here and there should meet with death, how better to disrupt a research program? They have learned their lesson as we learned it; they do not strike at the big public figures. But an obscure little man in Washington was run over by a truck six months ago, and, as a result, a million-dollar project had to retrace its steps quite expensively. A certain rocket specialist was shot to death on the West Coast, apparently by a drunken workman he had offended; a great deal of valuable information died with him. You have never heard of these men, very few people have. You have only heard of Amos Darrel because you happen to live in the same city, and the city happens to be close to Los Alamos, and his wife happens to collect literary and artistic figures as some women collect antiques. Yet Dr. Darrel is an important man in his line, and his death would mean a serious setback for the research he is directing. Do you wonder that, in desperation, certain people in Washington, remembering Mac's wartime work, summoned him and gave him authority to meet this threat ruthlessly, in his own way?" She wrinkled her nose. "It took them very long to reach this decision, of course. Washington is the city of the soft heads and the chicken hearts."

"And Amos?" I said.

"He would be dead now, quite possibly, if we had not reached him in time. She came well prepared, with a letter of introduction and a background of college journalism. What eminent man is going to deny a pretty girl with writing ambitions a few minutes of his time? They would have retired to a private room for the interview. There would have been a shot. Perhaps she would have fled 'through the window, or perhaps she would have been found standing over the body, dazed, gun in hand, with her hair disheveled and her dress torn." Tina shrugged. "There are many ways of doing it, as we know; or have you forgotten a certain General von Lausche? And operatives, even pretty female operatives, are always expendable. But we were there. And the girl recognized us and knew why we were there, and knew that she did not have long to live if she did not find a safe place to hide." Tina smiled. "Her manuscript would be her excuse, if you should come to the studio and find her. It is too bad that we deprived you of the scene she planned to perform for you. It would undoubtedly have been most interesting."

"Undoubtedly," I said. "So Mac is now running a kind of government bodyguard service?"

"Not exactly," Tina said. "There are two ways of giving protection, are there not? You can watch your subject day and night and hope to be alert enough to intercept or deflect the knife or bullet when it comes. Or you can identify and remove the would-be assassin. The police, the F.B.I., operate under a handicap. They cannot convict and execute a man for murder until he has murdered someone. Or a woman. We do not have this trouble. We hunt out the hunters. We execute the murderers before they commit their crimes."

"Yes," I said, turning the key in the ignition and putting my foot on the starter pedal. "Just one more thing. You're going to have to stay under cover for a while. Did you and Mac have a place in mind?"

Tina laughed softly, and leaned forward to place a hand on my knee. "But of course, my sweet," she said. "With you."

15

They build roads in New Mexico the normal way, except for one small aberration. After they've got the surface on, while it's still nice and soft, they give the signal to a drunk with a big disc harrow, who sets off at top speed along the fresh pavement, weaving artistically from side to side…

Well, maybe it doesn't happen that way, but I can think of no better explanation for the long, parallel, crooked furrows that decorate our southwestern blacktop roads. They aren't conspicuous. You probably don't even notice them in your softly sprung, balloon-tired Cadillac or Imperial, but in a truck with 6.00 x 16 tires inflated to thirty-five pounds it's like driving along a set of insane streetcar tracks laid by a madman for the sole purpose of throwing your heap into the ditch.

Along about dawn, I got tired of fighting the steering wheel and turned off onto a dirt road leading west across somebody's ranch. I followed this for a mile or two, until the growing light showed me a kind of hollow to the left where the desert cedars grew more thickly than elsewhere. I headed down there without benefit of road.

Parking in a little clearing among the low, twisted evergreens, I climbed out stiffly and eased the door closed without latching it, so as not to wake Tina, who was curled up asleep under her furs at the far end of the seat. Then I walked to the top of the nearest rise and stood looking at the brightening yellow-pink sky to the east. It was going to be another clear day. Most of them are, in our part of the country.

Little weak lights crawled across the dark plain under the beautiful sky, over where the highway was. I had that curious feeling of unreality you sometimes get after a sleepless night. It didn't seem likely that, some hundred-odd miles to the north, there was an abandoned mine containing a pretty girl with a sheathed throwing knife at the back of her neck and a bullet in her head—laid out neatly at the side of the black tunnel with a raincoat over her and her luggage beside her, and covered with as much protection in the way of rocks and earth as we'd been able to scrape together with the tools at our disposal. Tina had considered this a sentimental waste of time, and she'd been perfectly right, but I felt better for having done it. As she kept pointing out, I was soft, these days. I couldn't help thinking of things like rats and coyotes.

Nor did it seem very plausible that, only a few score yards from where I stood, there was sleeping a beautiful dark female in mink, who was not my wife…

I'm not a wood-fire enthusiast where cooking is

concerned, preferring just about any kind of stove if I can get it, but I hadn't got around to filling the can of white gas for the Coleman, and there was an autumn chill in the air and several dead trees around. We've got some kind of a bug that's been killing off the nice old evergreens at a fearful rate the last few years. I got out the axe, and presently I had a pleasant blaze going under the coffee pot and frying pan. I heard the cab door open. When I looked up, Tina was standing there, pushing the hair back from her face with both hands, stretching and yawning like a waking cat. I couldn't help laughing. She cut her yawn off short.

"What is funny, Eric?"

I said, "Baby, you should see yourself."

She looked down at herself in the light of the newborn day, and made a gesture as if to smooth down her clothing, but let her hands fall helplessly to her sides; the situation had obviously passed far beyond such simple remedies. She'd never again make a grand entrance in that particular outfit. Her gloves and hat were missing, already mere debris scattered about the truck. The smart black cocktail dress, its hem torn and dangling, was smeared with mine dust and creased with sleeping. Her pumps were rock-cut and grimy, and she had runs in both stockings. Only the furs about her shoulders seemed unaffected by the night's adventures. Their glossy perfection made the rest of her costume seem even more forlorn by comparison.

Tina laughed, and shrugged cheerfully. "Ah, well," she said, pushing her hair back from her face, *"c'est la guerre.*

You will buy me some new clothes when we come to a town, *nicht wahr*?"

"*Si, si*," I said, to prove I also knew some languages. "The dressing room is behind the third cedar to the west, and I hope you're a quick mover, because these eggs are almost done."

While she was gone, I spread an army blanket for us to sit on, dished up our breakfasts, and poured the coffee. When she came back, she'd combed her hair, pulled up her stockings, and put on some lipstick, but she still wasn't the most glamorous female in the world, even for five o'clock in the morning. The women's magazines to which Beth subscribes would have considered her case with pity and horror. She wasn't dainty, fresh, and sweet-smelling; it was clear that, in her present dilapidated condition, the poor girl had no chance whatever of attracting a man.

Sometimes I wonder where those mags get their data on male psychology. I ask you, gentlemen, is *your* beast generally aroused by a lovely lady looking like an angel and smelling like a rose? I'm not speaking of love and tenderness now; if you're looking for someone to protect and cherish, okay, and maybe that's what the female editors have in mind; but for purposes of passion, I think you want another stinking lowdown human being like yourself, not a shining and immaculate vision from above.

She sat down beside me. I handed her her plate, put her cup on a level spot beside her, cleared my throat, and said, "We left tracks all over those hills back there, but if anybody knows enough to look for them, and follow them to the mine, they know too much already. Do you want some whiskey in your coffee?"

She glanced at me. "Should I?"

I shrugged. "It's supposed to be good for warding off the chill, also for softening up members of the opposite sex for immoral purposes."

"Are your purposes immoral, *chéri*?"

"Naturally," I said. "I'm bound to be unfaithful to my wife before I'm through with you. It was inevitable from the moment I saw you last night. Well, this is a nice quiet place. Let's get it over with, so I can relax and stop wrestling with my conscience."

She smiled. "Somehow, I do not think you're wrestling very hard, my dear."

I shrugged and spread my hands. "It's not much of a conscience."

She laughed. "Your approach is so crude and I am so hungry. Wait until I've finished my breakfast before you rape me. But I will take a little whiskey in my coffee, thank you." She watched me pour it into her cup and mine. After a little, she said, "Your wife is very pretty."

"And very nice," I said, "and I love her dearly, in another existence, and now let's shut up about my wife. That's the Pecos River down the valley. You can't see it, but it's there."

"Indeed?"

"It's a very historic stream," I said. "There was a time when 'West of the Pecos' meant something wild and wonderful. Charles Goodnight and Oliver Loving were ambushed by Indians—Comanches, I think—not too far from here. They were taking a herd of Texas cattle north. Loving was wounded in the arm. Goodnight slipped away and came back with help, but Loving's arm got infected and he died from blood poisoning. The Comanches were great horsemen, some of the finest fighting men who ever drew a bow. I've never written much about them."

"Why not, *Liebchen*?"

"They were a great warrior nation. I can't dislike them enough to make them villains; and on the other hand, most books about noble redskins make me want to vomit, even my own. Now, the Apaches are much better suited to literary purposes. In their way, I suppose, they were kind of great, too—certainly they kept the U.S. Army running in circles for a hell of a long time—but they didn't have many admirable character traits that I can discover. As far as I can make out from the available records, the biggest thief and liar was the most highly respected Apache. Courage was for the birds, in their book. Oh, an Apache could die bravely enough if he absolutely had to, but it would always be a blot on his record: he should have been able to pull a sneak somehow. And their sense of humor was fairly gruesome. They liked nothing better than raiding a lonely ranch, eating the mules—they were very fond of mule meat—and leaving the inhabitants behind in what they considered a hilariously funny condition. I mean, take one prisoner, scalp well, chop off the ears and nose, gouge out the eyes and tongue, slice off the breasts if female and the private parts if male, and sever the heel tendons. Then, if they were Apaches of the old school— they're all civilized and respectable now, of course— they laughed themselves silly watching the bloody, croaking thing flopping blindly around in the dirt. Then they rode off, leaving it still alive, so that the next white man who came along, if he was merciful enough to take the responsibility on his soul, had to shoot it. This wasn't a ritual, you understand, not a ceremonial test of courage like the tortures of some other tribes. It was just a bunch of the boys having themselves some good clean fun. Oh, the Apaches were a wonderful, uninhibited people in their day. They kept New Mexico and Arizona practically deserts for years. They make fine heavies. I don't know how I'd make a living without them." I reached for her plate as she set it aside. "More?"

She shook her head, smiling. "You do not encourage the appetite, Eric. And you have a strange way of setting the mood for love, with this talk of gouged-out eyes and sliced-off breasts."

"I was just talking," I said. "Just showing off my vast store of specialized knowledge. A man's got to talk about something while he waits for a woman to feed her face. I'd rather talk about Apaches than about my wife and kids, as you were starting to do."

"It was you who mentioned her first."

"Yes," I said, "to keep the record clear, but you weren't

supposed to take the ball and run with it… What the hell are you doing?"

She looked a little startled by the question. She was lying back against a duffel bag with her dress bunched carelessly and much leg showing; and she'd been idly picking at one of her stockings with a sharp fingernail, and watching the resulting run, encouraged, travel in a pale streak over her knee and down her shin and instep, to vanish inside her dusty shoe. Even though the nylons were already past saving, it seemed like an immoral thing to do.

She moved her shoulders. "I… like the way it tickles. What does it matter? It is already ruined. Eric?"

"Yes?"

"Have you always loved me?"

I said, "I haven't thought about you for ten years, darling."

She smiled. "That is not the question I asked. One does not have to think, to love."

Then, although the morning was chilly, she took off her glossy furs and laid them carefully away on a far corner of the blanket. She turned back to face me in her rumpled sleeveless dress. The bare arms made her look very vulnerable at that temperature; I wanted to take her just to keep her warm. Her lips were a little parted, and her violet eyes, half-closed, looked both sleepy and bright, if such a thing is possible. Her meaning was clear. She had put aside the only thing she'd brought here that she cared to preserve. The rest, already in disrepair, did not matter; I needn't concern myself about it. I didn't.

16

I bought a pair of jeans, 24 waist, a denim shirt, 14 neck, a pair of white athletic socks, size eight, and a pair of blue Keds, size seven and a half—she was no real Cinderella where her feet were concerned. Then I bought two boxes of .22 Long Rifle High Speed cartridges and a bottle of bourbon. We were heading towards Texas, and although you won't believe it, that great big he-man state is practically dry. There are no bars, and the restaurants serve only beer and wine. Of course, there are ways of circumventing this strange legislation but... Texas, for God's sake!

The town wasn't large and they had all the stuff in one dark, dusty old general store—called a trading post out here—except the whiskey, for which I had to go to the shiny little drugstore across the street. Starting back towards the truck, I had to wait for a four-wheel-drive jeep station wagon to go by. It was one of the more recent glamorized jobs, green and white. Why anybody would bother to try to glamorize any kind of a jeep with two-tone paint I couldn't tell you. It seems kind of like tying a pink ribbon around the tail of a hardworking jackass.

There were two men in the front seat. One was an older man with a mustache. He was driving. The other was a young fellow in a big, flat-crowned black hat with the wide brim curving up at the sides—real cool, man. I couldn't see his feet, but his boots would have at least two-inch heels to go with that headgear, and his black leather jacket completed the ensemble perfectly.

I let the sturdy vehicle go past; then I crossed over, got into the truck, and drove out of town, heading south. It was getting close to noon now. We weren't going to set any mileage records for the day, having already wasted half the morning in one place—if you want to call it wasted. But then, we weren't going anywhere in particular; at least, if we were, I hadn't been informed of it yet. In the meantime, since no better itinerary had been offered me, I was sticking to my planned route down the valley of the Pecos.

It was a nice, bright day, with the sky clear blue, the land yellow-brown except for some distant purple mountains—the Sacramentos or Guadalupes—and the road black and clean and uncluttered by the herds of Texans and Californians who make our highways hideous during the tourist season. The Texans drive as if they own the country, the Californians as if they merely want to be buried in it, preferably with a few local yokels for company. But they'd all gone into hibernation for the year, and I cruised along at an easy sixty and grinned as I came up behind a little British car, on the rear of which was pasted a sticker reading: DON'T HONK, I'M PEDALING AS FAST AS I CAN.

I passed the little bug, jacked the speed up another five, and pretty soon found a dry creek bed crossing the highway, with a road—two wheel-tracks, rather—leading along it in the direction that would be upstream when the water was running. I turned in over a cattle guard and bounced along for a few hundred yards until a bend in the watercourse put some brush and cottonwoods between us and the highway—some, but not too much. There didn't seem to be anything of note around, except some Hereford steers, and they never bother anybody.

I got out and went into the bushes to pass the time convincingly, meanwhile watching the highway through the screen of brush and trees. The little import went buzzing past. Pretty soon the green and white jeep wagon came barreling along, containing only the mustached driver. I saw him start to turn his head as he went by, and think better of it; but he saw us all right, as he was supposed to. It wouldn't do for him to think we were hiding from him.

I went back to the truck, took Herrera's little revolver out of my hip pocket, and wedged it out of sight between the back and seat cushions. I'd been going to buy extra shells for that, too, and play around with it to see what it would do, but on second thought it had seemed better not to advertise that I had it. Sometimes an extra weapon, conveniently cached away, can be quite useful.

I went back and opened up the rear of the truck. Tina had made herself a kind of nest of duffel bags and bedding. She was lying there quite comfortably, wearing one of my old khaki shirts, open, and a black pantie-girdle that had survived the recent emotional storm with only minor damage.

Tina smiled at me. "This country of yours, *chéri!* One moment you are freezing, the next you are being roasted in a hot oven. Did you get me something to wear?"

I tossed her the paper-wrapped package. Looking at her, I felt a kind of constriction in my throat that had, I suppose, something to do with love, of one kind or another.

"I'm going up the wash and fire off a few rounds," I said. "Just to get my hand in. Come along as soon as you're ready, but don't rush it. Take everything nice and easy. We've been spotted, and we're probably being watched from up on the ridge right now."

Her eyes widened slightly. She looked at the cigarette she had been smoking, and pitched it past me, out the open door. "You are sure?"

I turned to grind out the smoldering stub with the toe of my boot. You get so it's a habit, particularly in a dry season, even when you're out on the desert where there isn't a damn thing to burn.

I said, "We've had an overgrown delinquent behind us in some kind of a jazzy Plymouth with fins like a shark, for the past fifty miles. Black hat and sideburns. Back in

town, he came rolling past in a jeep station wagon with
another fellow at the wheel. Now he's vanished, but the
jeep's on our tail. Pretty soon, I figure, the jeep will drop
out and another guy will take over in some other kind of
machinery, maybe a pickup for variety, and then perhaps
we'll go back to young Mr. Blackhat and his Plymouth
dreamboat." I reached out and patted her bare ankle,
which, slender and nicely formed, was worth a pat or two.
"Make it casual. Comb your hair and put on lipstick, out
where they can see you, before you join me."

"But, Eric—"

I said, "Just get dressed, honey, we'll talk later. If
they've got glasses on us, I don't want them to think
we're holding a council of war. I almost walked into the
side of their wagon, back in town, and they're probably
wondering if it was just a coincidence or if they've tipped
their hand."

I reached up to lower the canopy door. She said, "All
right, but leave it open, please, or I'll smother in here,
now that we've stopped."

I shrugged, and sauntered around to get the .22s out of
the cab. I wandered away upstream until I found a place
where the hank of the wash was steep enough to stop a
bullet without causing it to ricochet and endanger the
local cattle population, but not so high as to hide what
I was doing from any vantage points in the surrounding
territory that might be occupied by interested observers.
I set up a tin can, backed off about twenty yards, took
out the Woodsman, and emptied the clip, hitting with

seven out of the nine shots. Barbara Herrera had received the tenth bullet out of that load. I filled the clip and tried again, this time getting only one miss in ten shots. While I was shoving fresh cartridges into the clip, Tina came up, carrying a bundle.

I turned to look at her. She wasn't exactly the blue-jeans type as you see it portrayed locally. Her breasts and buttocks didn't threaten to erupt through the tough new cloth, which made her strictly a square, I guess, by current high-school standards. As a matter of fact, with her short black hair, she had kind of a boyish look.

"Everything fit?" I asked.

"The shirt is a little large," she said. "What do I do with this?"

She held out the bundle, which seemed to contain her discarded party clothes.

"Toss it into the bushes," I said, and grinned. "It'll give them something to investigate." She did as instructed. I offered her the gun. "Here. Shoot slowly and don't seem to pay much attention to me." I sat down on a boulder to watch her. She examined the pistol, shoved the safety off with her thumb, and fired once. "A couple inches low," I said. "Don't hold at six o'clock, she's sighted to shoot center… I know you'll have to report that we've got an escort, but an hour more or less isn't going to make too much difference. If we'd hung around that town long enough for you to scramble into some clothes and dash to the nearest phone, they'd have known we were on to them. I think it's better that we seem to be loafing along without a care in the world, so they feel they can take their time with whatever they plan to do—both here and in Santa Fe."

She fired again, and hit the can. "You do not think it can be the police?"

"It doesn't seem likely," I said. "There'd be no reason for them to keep us on ice like this. If the cops had something on us, they'd just move in and cart us off to jail. I think it's Herrera's bunch. The girl must have arranged to meet someone last night. When she didn't show, they set the wheels in motion."

"Yes," she said, "you may be right. But how did they find us?"

I waited for her to shoot and said, "I told them." She glanced at me quickly, surprised, and I said: "Me and my big mouth. I told Herrera at the party that I'd be heading down along the Pecos in the morning. She must have reported in before she came to the studio. When they missed her, they must have decided to try an intercept, gambling that I'd stick to my original route in order to make everything look natural and normal. They had plenty of time to get ahead of us while we were messing around back in the hills—anyway, the truck is no hot-rod. All they had to do was watch the one highway and pick us up as we went by." Tina fired again. I went on: "They know you're alive now. Therefore, even if they haven't found her, they must be almost certain Herrera's dead. Therefore they'll be assigning another operative to Amos Darrel."

Tina said, "And still you say we should be casual?"

"Yes," I said. "Because they don't know we know it, yet. They think we think we've got them fooled, so far, if you follow me. They think we think Amos is safe, for the time being. Which means that, rather than instituting a crash program, they'll probably let the new guy, whoever he may be, take a little time and set up the job right. Which gives Mac or whoever a little better chance of spotting him and taking him out of the play—as long as we keep these characters happy by shooting at tin cans and making love and in general acting like a couple of unsuspecting kids on a picnic."

Tina's next shot missed the can, as she glanced at me. "You mean you think they were watching…"

"It seems likely."

She laughed, but her face was slightly pink. "Why, the dirty Tom Peepers!" After a little, she said "But I must report. I must speak with Mac."

"Sure," I said. "They'll expect you to. After all, you've got to tell him that the body's safely buried, and that we've made a clean getaway, slick as a whistle. We'll stop for lunch pretty soon and let them see you put in the call. No harm in that, just as long as we take it easy and carefree."

She nodded, steadied the slim-barreled pistol, and emptied the rest of the clip rapid-fire. I could see the bullets striking in and around the can; she was no genius, either. We'd neither of us become famous for snuffing out candles at ten paces or shooting cigarettes out of people's mouths. I took back the gun, reloaded it, took her by the shoulders, and kissed her, saying, "We might as well give Mr. Peeper his money's worth."

"He's a dirty old goat," she said. "But let us give him his money's worth, by all means, *chéri*."

She moved abruptly, and I found myself, pushed and tripped at the same time, going over backwards. I landed in a sitting position almost hard enough to crack my pelvis.

"What the hell—"

"You great bully!" she cried, laughing at me. "You were so big and brave last night, catching me off guard when I was all dressed up and couldn't fight back. Kick my behind up behind my ears, will you?"

Her foot shot out. I tried to grab for it, but it was only a feint. She did some kind of a quick double-shuffle and, catching me on hands and knees—reaching, off balance—she put a foot in my rear and sent me forward on my face. Then she was running upstream, laughing. I picked myself up and charged after her. She was in better condition, but I had the longer legs and I was used to the altitude. She couldn't stay ahead of me. She tried to dodge, but the banks of the wash were steeper up here, and I caught her by an ankle as she scrambled for the top, and brought her back down in a little avalanche of loose dirt.

She twisted free, found her feet, and, as I closed with her incautiously, tried a wicked little chop to the neck that would have paralyzed me if I hadn't remembered the proper parry. She danced back out of reach.

"Slow!" she panted. "Just a great softy! I bet you do not even remember this one!"

Then we were working our way through the old hand-to-hand combat-and-mayhem routines, half seriously, holding back only enough so there would be no real damage if a blow should slip through. She was fast and in practice, and she had some new ones I'd never encountered. Finally she clipped me across the bridge of the nose hard enough to bring tears to my eyes, but she didn't get out again quite fast enough. I caught her, tied her up, threw her down, and pinned her. We were both gasping for breath in the thin desert air. I held her down until she stopped wiggling. Then I kissed her thoroughly; and when I was through, she lay there and laughed at me.

"Well, *Liebchen*?" she murmured. "What about Mr. Peeper and his money's worth?"

"You go to hell, you damn, nymphomaniac," I said, grinning.

"Old," she jeered, still lying there. "Old and fat and slow. Helm the human vegetable. Help me up, turnip."

I held out my hand to her, ready for a trick, and set my weight against hers as she tried to pull me off balance. I used her own effort to turn her around, and smacked her hard across the dusty seat of her jeans.

"Now behave yourself, Passion Flower," I said.

She laughed, and we buttoned ourselves up, tucked ourselves in, and brushed each other off. Then we walked back down the wash together. I felt oddly happy, with the guilty kind of happiness of a kid playing hooky from school. I'd been a good boy for years, my attendance record had been perfect, my deportment had been excellent, but it was all shot to hell now, and I didn't care. I was through being a model citizen. I was myself again.

17

In front of the restaurant, I put the truck into a slot next to a small, blue foreign sedan that I recognized, from the sticker on the back, the Texas plates, and other peculiarities, as the one I'd already passed on the road. It was a Morris. I'd read somewhere that they'd jacked up the horsepower from twenty-seven to a sizzling thirty-eight, but it still wasn't exactly what the sports-car boys like to call a bomb; you wouldn't have to worry about tearing up the pavement with the frantic acceleration when you let in the clutch. Glancing inside, I saw that the damn little heap, not much bigger than a perambulator, had a ducky little miniature air conditioning unit mounted under the dash. Well, that's Texas for you.

"It's a Morris," I said to Tina as I opened the truck door for her. "Remember the one we managed to promote in London, quite illegally, that I was always having to get out my Boy Scout knife on and dismantle that ridiculous electric fuel pump they must have got direct from the Tinker-Toy people."

"I remember," she said. "I was very impressed by your cleverness."

"You were supposed to be," I said. I gestured towards the public phone booth at the corner of the building. "Go ahead and do your stuff where everybody can see you. I'll wait for you inside. Got a dime?"

"Yes."

"Do you need more, or will Mac let you reverse the charges?" I grinned. "This peacetime operation must be the nuts. I can remember a few times in Germany when I'd have loved to pick up a phone and ask the boss what the hell to do next. Where do you get hold of him these days? Does he still have that hole in the wall just off 12th Street in Washington?"

I was just talking casually as we walked towards the building, to make us look bright and carefree. I didn't mean a thing by the questions, but Tina glanced at me sharply, and hesitated a long moment before she said in a half-embarrassed way: "I'm sorry, *chéri*. You know I can't give you information like that. I mean, you're not really… I mean, you've been outside a long time."

It was a little like being kicked in the teeth, although it shouldn't have been. After all, there would be quite a few of us alumni of Mac's unique institution of higher learning by this time. We couldn't all expect to be kept posted on developments back at the old alma mater.

"Yes," I said. "Sure, kid."

She put her hand on my arm and said quickly, "I'll ask him what… what your status is."

I shrugged. "Don't bother. You shoot 'em, I bury 'em. Unskilled labor, that's me."

She said, "Don't be silly, darling. Order me a hamburger and a Coca-Cola. By all means a Coca-Cola. One must drink the wine of the country, *nicht wahr*?"

"*Jawohl*," I said. "*Si, si. Oui, oui.* Roger."

"Eric."

"Yes."

Her eyes were apologetic. "I'm sorry. But you wouldn't tell me, if our situations were reversed. Not without instructions. Would you?"

I grinned. "Go make your call, and stop worrying about the morale of the troops."

Starting through the door, I drew back to make way for a young couple just coming out—a skinny young man in a sports jacket and the kind of checked cap that was once reserved for golfers, and a big horse of a girl in flat shoes, a tweed skirt, and a cashmere sweater. She damn well had to wear flat shoes. In high heels, she'd start having my trouble with low doorways.

For my courtesy, she smiled at me nicely, showing big, white, very even teeth. On second look, she was kind of attractive in a healthy and long-legged way. She reminded me of somebody, and I paused to watch her climb into the little blue car, fitting herself quite gracefully into the limited space. The man climbed in, and they drove off together, with the proud and self-conscious look of people who've found themselves something unique in the way of transportation.

It wasn't until I was inside the building that I realized who the girl reminded me of—my wife. Beth had once had that nice, young, well-bred, under-dressed, Eastern-girls-school look, just like this female Texas beanpole. Perhaps she still had it. It's a little hard to tell just how a girl looks after you've lived with her a dozen years or so. Well, Beth's looks weren't something I wanted to spend a lot of thought on, at the moment.

I picked up a Santa Fe paper from a stack of assorted news publications by the door and went on into the restaurant proper. It was done in chrome and Formica with plywood paneling, and it had all the warm and homelike atmosphere and authentic local color of a filling station, except that the waitresses wore full-skirted pseudo-Spanish costumes that reminded me a little of Barbara Herrera. I seemed to be in a reminiscent mood.

There was a big jukebox in the corner, on the democratic theory, I suppose, that a couple of dozen diners yearning for peace and quiet must not be allowed to frustrate the one minority screwball with a coin and a yen for noise. A beefy character in a gaudy shirt, high-heeled boots, and tight jeans that came up just high enough to cover his rump was feeding it some change, and as I wandered towards an empty table, the speaker let out a few weird sounds, and a man began to sing in an eerie, breathless voice about something coming out of the sky that had one big horn and one big eye.

I sat down and opened the paper and discovered that it was yesterday's, as might have been expected. Santa Fe has only an afternoon paper, and today's probably wouldn't get this far from home until supper time or later. It gave me a funny feeling to look at it, the same edition, to all appearances, as the one I'd picked up by the front door, glanced at, and tossed back into the house as we were leaving for the Darrels'—yesterday evening, before anything at all had happened. It seemed as if enough time had passed since then for them to print up a three-volume history of the era, let alone a new daily paper.

I folded the paper and looked around the room. A waitress sneaked up, stuck a menu and a glass of water in front of me, and escaped before I could trap her into taking the order. The jukebox was still going strong: the one-eyed, one-horned thing coming out of the sky had turned out to be a Purple People Eater, naturally.

Everybody in the place looked strange to me, all the peaceful people. I guess I was the thing coming out of the sky, with a knife in my pocket and a pistol under my belt and the dust of a secret grave still on my boots. I saw Tina come in, glance around, and start towards me, looking lean and competent in her jeans. She was another one, a carnivore among all the comfortable domestic animals. It was in her eyes and the way she walked, so obvious for a moment that I wanted to look around to see if anybody was staring at her with fear and horror.

I watched her come to the table, and it occurred to me that she wasn't a person in whom one could safely place one's childlike and innocent trust. None of us was. It occurred to me, also, that I'd have liked very much to talk with Mac myself, to get some idea where I stood. Not that I thought Tina might try to deceive me—I didn't think she might, I knew it. If the job required it, she'd lie unblushingly and ditch me without a qualm. Well, I'd have done the same to her. I'd done it to others when the occasion demanded; I had no kick coming.

She sat down opposite me, grimaced, and put her hands to her ears. "It should be illegal, to so torment innocent people."

I grinned. "What the hell do you know about innocent people?" She made a face at me, and I said, "At least they ought to let you buy five minutes of silence at the going rate. Did you get hold of Mac?"

"Yes," she said. "He says it's too bad we've been spotted. He says you were foolish to take a route you had already talked about."

"He does?" I said. "The next time, suppose he figures it out and sends me a routing in advance."

She shrugged. "Anyway, it's done. He's arranging for extra precautions to be taken in Santa Fe. Amos Darrel will be protected night and day until Herrera's replacement is identified and disposed of. Meanwhile, Mac agrees that your plan is the best, under the circumstances. We are to proceed happily on our way, looking neither to the right nor to the left, but nevertheless making an effort to identify those who follow us, so that they can be picked up when the time is ripe."

"We're to act as bait, eh?"

"Precisely, my love. And as for you," she said, "he asks are you planning to come back to us permanently? If so, he will tell you everything you need to hear when he sees you, which will be soon enough. If not, the less you know the better."

"I see."

She watched me across the table. "You must make up your mind, first. That is logical, is it not? Mac says there is a place for you, if you want it. You would have to take a refresher course of training, you understand, and you would not, at first, have quite the position of seniority you occupied at the end of the war. After all, there are people with us who have worked steadily for all the years the organization has been in existence… In the meantime, do not be hurt if I tell you nothing that is not essential to our present work. That will make it simpler for everybody, if you should decide to go back to your peaceful vegetable existence after all."

I said, "Yes. Of course, it depends a little on whether my peaceful vegetable existence will take me back."

Tina smiled. "Oh, she will take you back, my dear, if you are suitably humble and remorseful. After all, it is a very well-known situation: the old wartime love affair flaming into sudden life years later, flaming briefly and dying and leaving only the bitter ashes of disillusionment and regret. She will understand; secretly she will value you more for knowing that another woman has found you attractive—although she will never admit that, of course. But I do not think she will send you away, if you return humbly, asking forgiveness. So the decision is still entirely yours."

I shook my head. "Not entirely."

"What do you mean?"

"I mean, there are a few people around who aren't very fond of us, remember? There's a death to be paid for, and, as I recall, we used to make a point of paying those debts whenever possible, as a matter of principle. It seems unlikely they'll be more lenient. Anyway, we're bait, kid, and bait is always expendable. Let's not worry about my future until we're sure I've got one."

18

San Antonio was a big surprise to me. Remembering the sprawling, smog-bound horror the supposedly somewhat civilized Californians have perpetrated, under the name of Los Angeles, in a coastal region that must have been quite beautiful to start with, I hadn't really been looking forward to seeing what a bunch of crude Texans had managed to cook up in a rather arid and unpromising corner of their native state.

What I found was a nice old city with some of the unfortunate trappings of what's known as urban progress, but also with a better than average nucleus of pleasant old crooked streets and picturesque old buildings and plazas; and with a pretty river wandering through the busiest business section, rather like a toddler turned loose in Daddy's office. We drove around a bit to let me get the feel of the place, and I tried to act like a writer looking for material. We finally located the hotel we'd called for reservations, near the historic Alamo.

The uniformed doorman didn't bat an eye at the sight of my 1951 truck with its businesslike snow tires, camping canopy and spare water and gas cans. It's one of the advantages of traveling west of the Mississippi: you can drive something practical without being sent around to the service entrance.

After getting settled in our room, and cleaning up a bit we went out on foot to have another look at the town. I hung a camera around my neck, thinking to get some shots of the Alamo and other points of interest, but instead I spent the afternoon helping Tina pick out a skirt-and-blouse outfit for traveling and a sexy dress to wear out to dinner. This is supposed to be a hell of an ordeal for a man, but I don't see why it should be. To have an attractive woman—one you've made love to and expect to make love to again—parade herself before you in a variety of seductive dresses, asking for your approval, can be very interesting, kind of like the love dance of the peacock in reverse. Anyway, if you're going to have to look at her, why pass up the chance to exercise some control over her appearance?

The dress we got was sexy all right. She modeled it for me again that evening while I was tying my tie. It was soft, white wool, with a high neck and long sleeves. I put the mink about her, turned her around, and looked her up and down. She didn't seem to have much slack.

"Can you walk," I asked, "or should I get a bellboy with a dolly and have him trundle you to the elevator?"

She laughed. "It is better than those jean pants, *hein*?

Now you may kiss me, but do not muss me—that we will save for later. First we will eat and get comfortably drunk. What is the name of this place you were told about?"

"I've got it written down," I said. "Don't ask me to pronounce it. I never could handle French gracefully, not even when my life depended on it, and that was quite a while ago... Tina?"

"Yes, *chéri*?"

"Did you get the impression we were followed this afternoon?"

She glanced at me. "I do not think so. It was hard to tell, walking, with all the traffic. If it was done, it was done well, by many different people. Did you see anyone?"

I shook my head. "No familiar faces. Well, maybe they've been called off. I wonder..."

She patted my cheek. "Wonder tomorrow. Not tonight. This is a nice town and we are going to have a fine time."

"Sure," I said. "But I could relax a lot better if Mac would turn up and give me the answer to a few simple questions."

The recommended place turned out to be small and exquisite and very, very French. They provided setups for the whiskey I'd brought along in a paper-wrapped bottle, Texas style. If you spent a lot of time in the state, I reflected, it would almost pay you to invest in a flask. I learned that Tina had developed into quite a gourmet since I'd last known her. She went into a huddle with the waiter, the head-waiter, and the wine steward, all of whom loved her because she could speak perfect French—and, of course, the fact that she wasn't bad to look at in that white dress didn't turn them against her. They settled upon roast capon with mushrooms. A capon, I gathered, is to a rooster what a steer is to a bull. In theory, it hardly seemed worth while to go to all that trouble for a mere chicken; in practice, the idea proved to have a lot of merit. The wine, I was told, was a special vintage from a certain great year, I forget which one. All in all, it was quite a production, and one that threw some doubt on my mental picture of Texans as a people living exclusively on tough range beef. To be sure, the stuff was being cooked and served by Frenchmen, but the natives around us seemed to be putting it down with enthusiasm.

We'd arrived in a taxi, since it seemed simpler and more elegant than getting the truck out of hock. Riding back, we did not speak for a while. Then I wriggled uncomfortably.

"What is the matter, *Liebchen*?"

"This damn big bottle," I said, pulling it out of my coat pocket. I laid it aside. Then I turned and drew her to me and kissed her hard.

Presently—but not immediately, by any means—Tina made a small sound of protest and drew away.

"Please, darling!" she whispered breathlessly. "Remember that you must leave me in condition to walk through the lobby of that respectable hotel past all those respectable people!"

I said, "The hell with respectable people. Let's tell the guy to drive through the park for a while. They've got to have a park in this town, somewhere."

I was kidding, I guess, but with whiskey and wine to encourage me, I don't suppose I'd have backed down if she'd agreed, even though the back seat of a taxi would surely have cramped my style. She hesitated a moment, considering the idea with real interest; then she laughed, took my face in her hands, kissed me on the mouth, and pushed me away.

"Ah, we are not children," she said. "We have the dignity and the self-control. We can wait a few minutes. Besides, I do not really think there is room here."

I grinned, and she laughed again, and raised herself from the seat so that she could tug her dress down where it belonged. She rearranged her furs, and drew me close to her. "It is not so far now," she said. "Eric."

"Yes."

"I waited for you. After the war. Why did you not come?"

I didn't answer at once. Then I said, "I could lie and say I couldn't make it because I was in the hospital. But it wouldn't be true."

"No," she said. "You met a girl, did you not. And she was sweet and soft and innocent, and she had never seen a dead man, except perhaps in an antiseptic hospital bed."

"That's right," I said. "And I told Mac I was quitting, and I married her and deliberately put it all behind me, you with the rest."

"Yes," she said. "It was what you should have done. It was what I would have wished for you, my dear. And now I have spoiled it."

"Maybe," I said. "But you had some help from me."

She was silent for a while. Presently she took out a handkerchief and turned my face towards her and scrubbed my mouth. Then she took out comb and lipstick and worked on herself for a while. She held the purse up a little longer, studying the mirror.

"I wonder," she said, "if you *had* come for me… Well, it is no use wondering, is it?"

"Not much," I said.

She said, "You know, of course, that we are being followed again."

"Yes," I said. "I've been watching him in the driver's mirror." I glanced at the headlights reflected in the rectangle of glass up forward. "I'd say they've been giving us a little leeway, hoping to throw us off guard. Now they should be about ready to close in."

19

The car that had been following us went on when we made the turn for the hotel entrance. It was the jeep station wagon we'd met before, or its twin sister.

"They're playing this real cute. Now you see them, now you don't," I said, getting out and turning to help Tina to the sidewalk. "Somebody's being too clever for words."

"It would seem so, *chéri*," Tina said. She smoothed down her dress. "It is a pity I look so much better in narrow skirts," she said. "They are such a nuisance when one has to run or fight... Eric."

"Yes?"

"If something should happen. If we should become separated now, in one way or another—"

I glanced at her sharply, wondering what she had in mind. "Don't get corny," I said.

"No. Let me say it. There may come a time when you will hate me for what I have done to you. Just remember, my dear, that I had no choice. None of us has a choice. Not really."

Her violet eyes were dark and grave and very lovely; but it seemed, on the whole, like a hell of a time for deep thoughts.

"Yes," I said, after a moment. "Sure." I remembered the taxi driver, and turned and paid him. As he drove off, I swung back to Tina. "Well, we can't stand here all night... Damn!"

"What is it?"

"I forgot that lousy bottle." The cab was just turning the corner. I sighed and let it go. "Well, there's a taxi driver who ought to have a happy night," I said, and accompanied Tina across the sidewalk towards the hotel doorway. "Just one thing, sweetheart. One question."

"Yes?"

"Which of us calls the signals if something breaks?"

She hesitated. "You may call them, Eric."

"All right," I said. "You've said it. Now keep it in mind and don't get independent." I laughed suddenly. "You know something, it occurs to me that we're almost legitimate, for a change. It's the first time I've ever been in a spot like this when I could even consider calling on the local police for help."

Tina smiled and shook her head. "I do not think it would be a very good idea. I do not think Mac would approve. He does not like explaining our activities to unsympathetic policemen more frequently than is absolutely necessary."

I said, "Well, if the party gets rough, he may have to do some explaining whether he likes it or not. I'm not going to stand still for being shot or beat up just to save him a little breath… Watch it now!" I breathed. "Eyes front, honey. Laugh and be merry."

We were inside, entering the lobby. It was the usual great, pillared, carpeted hall sprinkled with groups of chairs and sofas that, although similar in design, did not seem to have been formally introduced to each other. One wall was glass, looking out upon a patio with dense, flood-lighted, tropical vegetation. Here and there were the lobby-sitters you find in any hotel at practically any hour of the day or night. Why they choose to read their books and newspapers in a drafty lobby instead of a comfortable hotel room I couldn't tell you. Maybe they're all waiting for someone, but if so, why doesn't that person ever show up?

None of the characters I could see sitting around was a day under fifty, except one. I laughed and put my arm about Tina's waist as we started down the long room. Her answering laughter was a little slurred, and she leaned against me, as if for support.

"Where?" she asked softly.

I laughed again, as if she had suggested something immoderately funny. "Second sofa on the left, looking out towards the patio. Female, young, close to six feet tall, light brown hair, brown tweed suit."

"How can you tell how tall she is, *Liebchen*, when you can only see the back of her head?"

"We've met her before, with an Ivy-League-looking punk in a golf cap, driving a little Blue British Morris with a funny sign on the back. Remember, the restaurant where you made your call to Mac? They were just coming out the door as I went in. You were heading for the phone booth, maybe you didn't notice them."

Tina giggled in an inebriated way that contrasted strangely with her calm voice: "I did not, but I will take your word."

"She might just be here to keep an eye on us," I said, "but I've got a hunch she's the finger. Five gets you twenty that as soon as we've turned the corner she'll head for the house phones to let them know we're on the way up."

"Then you think they're waiting for us up in the room?"

"It seems likely."

She hesitated. "So?"

I kissed her on the ear as we walked. "So, we should have made love in the taxi like I said. Looks like we're going to be a little too busy now."

She laughed softly. "I do not think you have your mind concentrated on important things."

I said, "With you practically crawling into my pants pocket, how can I?" I drew a long breath, and let the kidding go. I said, "Let's give them a surprise. I'm tired of being the mouse end of this cat-and-mouse routine."

"Eric, we are not supposed to make unnecessary trouble."

"What's unnecessary? Something's cooking. I don't

like to play other people's games."

She leaned her head sleepily on my shoulder as we walked along the soft carpet, close together, "You are sure of this girl?"

I said, "It's the same girl. It could be coincidence, running into her again."

"If she uses the telephone, that will be confirmation."

"She's not going to use the telephone," I said. "She's not going to get anywhere near a telephone. We're taking her now."

We were passing the back of the girl's sofa; I could have reached out with my left hand and patted her smooth brown hair. She was engrossed in a copy of *Harper's*. She wasn't watching our reflections in the glass wall in front of her, of course. She had no interest in us at all, but I was willing to bet that, no matter how well they'd trained her, she felt a little crawling sensation at the back of her neck as we went past. Only we didn't go past.

We walked around the end of the sofa and stopped in front of her. "Why, hello, there!" I said cheerfully.

She did it very well. She looked up casually, decided that I must have been addressing somebody else since she didn't know me, and looked, back down at her magazine. Then she looked up a second time, with a puzzled frown.

"I beg your pardon."

She was really quite nice-looking, in a tall and tweedy and young sort of way, and, although she was a much bigger girl, she still reminded me obscurely of Beth. She was still wearing low-heeled shoes, I noticed, but her long legs were fine, nevertheless. She had the lean, clean look of a good photographer's model. To read, she had put on glasses with thick, dark rims. She took them off now to look at me.

"I beg your pardon?" she said again, making a question of it this time.

Tina was already sitting on the sofa beside her, and Tina's hand had slipped into the secret pocket of the mink stole. I didn't like that too well. This was no place for firearms.

Tina said, "You didn't tell us you were coming to San Antonio, dear."

I said, "We've got to celebrate this reunion. I'd say the bar, if we weren't in Texas, and if I hadn't left our bottle in the taxi. But there's still part of a fifth in my suitcase upstairs."

"Well, that's all right," Tina said. She spoke to the girl. "You will join us in a drink up in our room, won't you, dear?"

The girl's face was blank. "I'm sorry. There must be some mistake."

I was sitting on her left now. I took my hand out of my pocket. The knife made a small click as I opened it. The girl looked down quickly. I drove the blade into her side, holding it with thumb and forefinger to measure the proper depth: just enough to penetrate clothing and skin and an eighth to a quarter of an inch of flesh. Her eyes went wide, her mouth opened, and her indrawn breath was a soft, hissing gasp. She made no other sound.

"Just a short one," I said. "For the road."

"Who are you?" she whispered, holding herself rigid and unmoving, braced against the pain of the knifepoint in her side. "What do you want?"

I said, "We're just some people who want you to have a drink with us, up in our room."

"But I don't understand—" Her eyes were hurt and bewildered and scared. She was very good. She licked her dry lips. "I'm sure," she said, "there must be some terrible misunderstanding."

"Not yet," I said. "But it could happen any time. I might even get the idea you were refusing to cooperate, even though you had no such thought in mind. That would be too bad, wouldn't it? Let's go, Shorty."

We had no trouble at all. The elevator was on the ground floor when we reached it, and the attendant took us up without giving us a second look.

"All right," I said to the girl, as the doors closed behind us and the cage went up to answer a call at another floor. "All right, no more knives, Shorty. There are two guns behind you now. You can turn your head and check this if you like." She hesitated, and looked around slowly. Her glance moved from Tina's little Browning to my Colt .22 to my face.

"What—" She licked her lips again. "What do you want me to do?"

I said, "It's entirely up to you. We're going to room 315, down the hall to the left, there. You're going to open the door and walk in. If you want to knock a certain way, first, that's all right. If you want to say something to whoever's inside, that's all right, too. But you're going in ahead of us, and the first shot that's fired, if anything at all happens, will be me shooting you."

"What makes you think there'll be somebody in your room? What in Heaven's name makes you think I—"

I said, "If I'm wrong, I'll certainly apologize all over the place later."

"But I swear to you, I don't know anybody in San Antonio except my husband. I was waiting for him to join me when you came along!" The tears in her eyes were as real and as perfect as diamonds. "You're making a terrible mistake!"

I said, "So, if I'm making a mistake, there'll be nobody in the room, and nobody'll get hurt. Let's go find out, shall we?"

She started to speak, but checked herself, and drew a long, uneven breath, and turned away from me. We went around the corner and down the hall. Tina was beside me. The girl walked, very straight, before us. She stopped at the door.

"You said… you said 315?"

"Yes," I said. "Give her the key, Tina."

Tina put the key into her hand. "Eric, are you sure—"

"Who's sure?" I said. "Tomorrow, the sun may rise in the west."

The girl said, "You want me to open the door?"

"That's the idea," I said. "But any signals or counter-signs you want to give first—"

"Oh, stop it!" she cried. "You sound like a bad movie! You sound like… I don't know any secret signals, I assure you! Shall I open it or not?"

"Go ahead," I said. "Open it. Walk straight in. You can't throw yourself aside fast enough that I'll miss you with my first shot. It's been tried."

She said, breathlessly, "I haven't the slightest intention of making a sudden move, so please be careful with that trigger… Well, here I go, if you're quite ready."

I didn't say anything. She hesitated, clearly hoping I'd speak again to delay the moment; then she sighed and put the key into the lock. As she turned it, I reached past her with my foot and kicked hard. The door slammed back. I had the girl by the collar of her tweed jacket. I shoved her straight forward. She was a nice-looking kid, but if anybody was going to get shot, it wasn't going to be me, if I could help it.

There were no shots. The room was empty.

I pushed the girl away from me so hard that she stumbled and had to cling to the foot of the nearest bed to keep from falling. I swung around so that I could cover the bathroom, but the door was open there; it was a small place, and I could see that there was nobody inside. I heard Tina move behind me.

"Close the door!" I said without turning my head. I heard it close. "Lock it!" I said.

Nothing happened. The girl was crouching, on one knee by the bed, watching me. There was a funny, surprised expression on her face. She looked frightened half to death, and at the same time she looked as if she wanted to laugh.

"Tina," I said without turning my head. Nobody answered. I backed away from the kneeling girl, far enough so she couldn't reach me in one lunge. I looked around. There was nobody behind me. Tina was gone.

20

I backed to the door and put my hand on the knob. I thought I could hear the sound of quick, light footsteps in the hall outside, hurrying away, but the girl in the tweed suit started to rise and I had to give her my attention. A lot of good men have died as the result of not taking an attractive female adversary quite seriously. I didn't intend to be one of them.

"Hold the pose," I said. "If you move, you're dead." She froze, looking at the slim-barreled .22 aimed directly at her. I took a chance and yanked the door open left-handed. Nothing happened. The corridor was empty, except for two objects lying just beyond the threshold of the room: the tall girl's brown leather purse and her copy of *Harper's,* both of which Tina had been carrying.

They told the story completely. If Tina had been silently overpowered behind my back and whisked away—which seemed implausible in any case—she'd have dropped her own purse as well, not to mention the gun she'd been holding. No, it was no time for me to be kidding myself. Tina had pulled out, tossing aside the unwanted purse and magazine as excess baggage in her voluntary flight. I crouched, picked them up, dropped them on a nearby chair inside, pulled the door closed again, and locked it.

"She ran out on you," the tall girl said maliciously, still balanced on one knee by the end of the bed. "I saw her. I saw the look on her face. She'd had enough of you, she was saving her own skin. I don't blame her. But now she's gone I want to tell you—"

"I don't want you to tell me anything," I said. "Keep your trap shut until I say otherwise. You may stand up now."

"Yes, sir." She got to her feet.

"It isn't necessary to acknowledge the instructions. Just follow them... Now take one step away from that bed and hold it. Did you ever pose for photographs professionally?"

Her eyelids flickered. "Why, yes."

"I thought so," I said. "I've taken enough pix myself to recognize the type... Then there's no excuse for your not standing perfectly still, is there?"

She said, "You've got to listen to me. I'm not—"

I said, "I'm going to tell you just once more. Shut up. Or comes it a gun-barrel in the teeth." She started to speak. I raised the pistol slightly. She checked herself. "That's better," I said. I reached back to pick up her purse. It contained no weapon. "Mary Frances Chatham,"

I said, glancing through the identification cards. "Mrs. Roger Chatham."

She started to speak again, thought better of it, and stood with her lips compressed, despising me. I tossed the purse back on the chair and stood looking at her thoughtfully, reviewing in my mind everything that had happened since we entered the room. I didn't think I'd had my eyes off her long enough for her to have got rid of anything she was carrying, but there was no sense in taking chances.

"Take another step forward and hold it," I said.

"May I?"

"What?"

"It's an old game," she said. "Children play it. It's called Giant Step. You have to ask 'may I' before you move."

It was too bad. I'd warned her. If she'd been a man, she'd have got it squarely across the mouth as I'd promised. Since she was a girl—a girl who looked just a little like my wife—I clipped her above the ear, instead. She swayed, and started to raise her hand to the side of her head, but remembered the gun, and stopped the risky movement. When she looked at me again, her gray eyes were wet with pain. I was giving her a bad time. Well, I wasn't having much fun myself.

I said, "Mrs. Chatham, I once spent four hard years at this business. I know all about the technique of chattering brightly to distract the opposition. I can't afford to believe anything you tell me, so I don't intend to waste time listening to it. The next time you open your mouth without being asked, you'll lose some teeth. Is that clear?" She didn't speak. I repeated: "Is it clear?"

"Yes," she whispered, hating me. "Yes, it's clear."

"All right. Now, one step forward without comments. If you please."

She took the step. That put her far enough from the bed so I could search all parts of it she could have reached without being within too easy range of any tricks she might know. I suspected that, with her physique, given an opening, she'd be as hard to handle as lots of men who thought they were really tough. I didn't find anything hidden in the bed.

I straightened up, frowning. There were two separate problems involved. There was the problem of Tina's sudden defection, if that was what it was—and now that I thought about it, it occurred to me that she'd kind of made a point, earlier, of saying: goodbye, don't hate me. In the long run, this might be the more serious problem, but for the moment I thought I could pass it up. I'd just have to figure the immediate play without Tina, that was all.

Then there was the problem of the girl before me and the man behind her—because somewhere in the background, I knew, there was a man, a very smart and dangerous man, thinking very clever thoughts. I'd underestimated him seriously once tonight, when I'd assumed he'd set a simple and obvious trap here. I couldn't afford to make the same mistake again. He had something more complicated in mind. I didn't have too much time left to figure out what it was.

I looked at the girl again. Well, it was the logical next step. I said, "Strip."

"What?"

"Take it off. Remove it. Peel."

"But—"

I shifted the gun to my left hand, and reached in my pocket for the knife. I flicked it open one-handed, grasping the exposed part of the blade and giving that quick snap of the wrist that lets the weight of the handle carry it open. "No," I said as the girl's eyes widened, "I'm not going to threaten you. I don't have to. I've skinned rabbits. I've skinned deer. I've skinned bear, moose, and elk. Any man who's wrestled a bull-elk hide ought be able to dispose of a tweed suit, a sweater, and some assorted nylon junk. Of course, the clothes aren't likely to be much good to you after I get through cutting them off you."

We stared at each other for several seconds; then her glance dropped and she unbuttoned and pulled off her jacket, hesitated, and laid it on the rug at her feet. Reluctantly, she unzipped and unhooked the fastenings at the side of her skirt. I put the knife away and got the gun back into my right hand. I used to be a passable shot with my left hand, too—we all had to be—but that was a long time ago.

"Just let it fall and step out of it," I said as she still stood there, clinging to her opened, sagging skirt. "Keep working, I haven't any designs on your white body, Mrs.

Chatham, but I'm apt to get some if you keep teasing me like this."

She flushed, and hurried up the rhythm of her undressing. As might have been expected from her low heels and tweedy outer garments, her lingerie was as unglamorous as could be found outside a men's wear department. There was no lace or embroidery, there were no little pleated nylon ruffles to tickle Mr. Chatham's fancy, if there was a Mr. Chatham and if he had a fancy. Probably his name was Joe Jones, he liked small blondes, and he was just along for the ride, on orders.

When we got down to it, her figure was quite admirable, although it was, if you'll pardon the expression, a studio figure rather than a bedroom figure. It made my fingers itch, but only for a camera.

"All right," I said, "come away from your clothes. Over here." She obeyed, and tried to confront me defiantly, but she couldn't look me in the face. Well, it was kind of nice to meet one who was self-conscious about her body, for a change… I checked that line of thought. Tina was gone. There wasn't anything to be gained by being bitter, at least until I knew for sure I had something to be bitter about. "Lock your hands behind your back," I said to the girl. "Okay, now bend towards me. If those hands let go of each other, I'll club you down."

She bent forward, and I ran my fingers through her light-brown hair. I found only a small lump over her ear that I had put there. There was nothing taped to her scalp. There was nothing under her armpits or in any of the other crevices of her body. I don't know where they got her, she was almost à pathological case. She'd have to get over it before she could be trusted with serious work. In other respects, she'd done quite well, but who can use an operative, male or female, who can't stand being searched without half dying of embarrassment?

I made her place her hands flat against the wall, leaning well forward, and hold that position precariously while I searched her clothes. If she was carrying so much as a cyanide capsule, it was too well hidden for me to find without methodically dissecting her outfit, seam by seam, and it wasn't that important. She was certainly packing no major weapon, not even a razor-blade.

"All right, Mrs. Chatham," I said. "You may cover it up now." She didn't seem to catch on right away. I said gently, "It's all right, Shorty. The nightmare is over. Put your things back on."

She didn't speak until she'd got dressed as far as her slip, a very plain and practical white garment. Then, with enough clothes on to give her courage again, she glanced at me quickly. "I hope somebody does shoot you!" she breathed. "I hope they're careful, so you don't die too fast. And now go ahead and hit me for talking without permission!"

I said, "It's all right. Blow off steam if you want to. You're pretty good, you know, but you've got to get over dying of shame just because some guy who doesn't give a damn sees you with your clothes off... I mean, just a little advice from one pro to another."

She said, "What makes you think I'm a—"

"You made two mistakes, Mrs. Chatham. Or let's say you made the same mistake twice."

"I don't know what you're talking about!"

I said, "Despite what you're thinking of me, I'm not really a sadist. I don't jab pretty girls with knives just for kicks."

Her eyelids flickered. Practically everybody's got some little give-away, particularly the young ones who need further instruction. This was hers. She rubbed her side with her forearm, where I'd stuck her. "What do you mean?"

"I mean," I said, "it was a test and you failed it, Shorty. You should have screamed. A nice, innocent, sheltered young girl, suddenly stuck with a knife, would have jumped six feet in the air and yelled bloody murder, even in the middle of a hotel lobby. She couldn't have helped herself. And when I smacked you with the gun-barrel, you didn't clap your hand to the spot—the normal reaction. Oh, you started to, all right, but you remembered that there was a weapon covering you and that if you made a sudden move I might get nervous and shoot. After a painful crack on the head, no untrained young bride from the country would have remembered that, or had the self-control to act on it… It's the old Trojan-Horse routine, isn't it?"

I watched her eyes. There was that little twitch of the lids that she'd have to learn to control, now that she was in the big time.

She licked her lips. "I don't know what you mean. If you'd only listen to me—"

The telephone rang. She didn't look at it right away; she wasn't that good. You can't wait for something through intolerable ages of fear and humiliation, and then act quite naturally when it happens. But if she hadn't been expecting it, she'd have jumped at the first ring.

We stood there, facing each other, and let the instrument tinkle away on the table between the beds. After the fifth ring it fell silent.

I said, "The old Trojan-Horse routine, and very cleverly done, too. The purpose being to get an accomplice into the enemy camp, somehow. First they showed us a car we'd recognize, following us. That put us on the alert. Then they showed us you, sitting there. I'd seen you yesterday, so I'd be sure to recognize you. What would I do when I saw you? Well, I might lose my nerve and try to make a run for it—they'd have to allow for that possibility. But I might also, being a bold and impetuous character, do something direct and melodramatic, like walking right up to you and taking you along for a hostage or a source of information. If I did, fine. Where would I bring you? Why, up here, of course. Where else in San Antonio could I go?"

She was silent. All around us the hotel was silent, but I could feel them closing in. There wasn't much time left.

"Up here," I said. "Why they chose to move in on us in the middle of a big city full of people and policemen, I don't know, when they could have taken us out in the open, but they've undoubtedly got their reasons. And up here you'd put on the big innocence act until we weren't quite sure we hadn't made a mistake. We'd find that you were unarmed and presumably harmless—no girl who can blush all over can be anything but harmless, can she? And then the telephone would ring. If I picked it up, it would be a wrong number, but it wasn't the wrong number to you. It was the signal to tell you to get ready. And then there'd be a knock on the door, threatening voices perhaps, or just a key in the lock, and as we turned that way, forgetting all about you, you'd whip a gun from somewhere and have us covered from behind... Somewhere?" I looked around the room. "But where, Mrs. Chatham? Where did they cache the gun for you, while we were out to dinner? Or did they? Why hide a gun that might be found and tip off the play, when there was already one handy, as they'd discover soon enough, looking the place over in our absence. All they had to do was tell you where it was."

Still watching her, I moved sideways towards the big chair by the window. Her eyelids betrayed her again, as my hand dipped down behind the cushion and came up with the snubnosed revolver I'd hidden there earlier in the day, the gun that had once belonged to Barbara Herrera.

Her face had changed. When she spoke, so had her voice. It was older and stronger and firmer than it had been. She was no longer a scared young bride trapped in a terrifying and incomprehensible situation, but then, she never had been. "Mr. Helm…"

I grinned briefly. "So you know my name."

"Of course I know your name!" she said quickly, "I know your other one, too: Eric. I've been trying to tell you... Yes, yes, you're quite right about me, but you've got to listen, you can't—"

It was the same old desperate last-minute chatter. They won't let you do it in golf, to make the guy miss his putt, or in trap-shooting or target shooting or chess, but we've got no rules of sportsmanship in our racket; you can talk all you want to, if the guy's fool enough to let you. It made no difference at all what she had to say. It might be the pure, golden, 18-carat truth, but it probably wasn't, and I had no time to run an assay on it.

I said, "If you go over by the door and lie down against the wall, I'll try not to hit you with any stray bullets when your friends break in."

She said fiercely, "You don't understand! You're making a terrible mistake, you've got to listen to me! It's not what you think, you mustn't start shooting—"

"Who's starting anything?" I said. "If nobody comes through that door, nobody'll be hurt. If you want them alive, just call them off."

"I can't," she cried, "I can't, they're already—"

Somebody put a key in the lock. I drew a long breath, held it, and steadied the two guns. I felt it come, the thing that had been missing since the war, the thing that's very close to sex, except that it deals in death instead of life. The girl was staring at me as if I'd suddenly grown twelve feet tall, and perhaps in a sense I had. A man is always just a little bigger when he's ready to kill.

"Come on, boys," I murmured, watching the door. "Come to papa! Come and get it!"

Mary Frances Chatham threw a desperate glance towards the opening door, shouted a cry of warning, and launched herself directly at me. I'd expected that. It was no problem. She had yards to go, and I was ready for her…

She was dead, you understand. It was all over. She was on the floor with a bullet in her brain. There wasn't anything left to do but cart her out and plant her. It was all taken care of, just a distraction from the main business, and I was thinking ahead, about the opening door and how to take care of the first man through so he'd make the most trouble for the guys behind… And then I discovered that I hadn't shot at all. I was still standing there, watching foolishly as she came driving at me like a Notre Dame fullback with goal to go. The sights were steady, the target was clear, and I couldn't pull the damn trigger. I suppose it was the years of peace that betrayed me—that, and the fact that she did look just a little like Beth.

She hit me hard, drove me back against the wall by the window, and tied me up with a kind of suicidal frenzy. It was no longer a question of not shooting her, it was a question of keeping her from shooting herself with one of the guns I was holding. Behind her, the door swung fully open, and Mac came in.

21

I recognized him instantly, of course; he wasn't a man you forgot. But there was a wild and crazy moment when I couldn't understand what he was doing there. All kinds of fantastic possibilities went through my mind in the space of a second or two. Then I made the logical connection: Tina had slipped away, Mac was here. It added up right, and it made me feel fine. I hadn't allowed myself to speculate too much about Tina's disappearance; but I discovered that it was a pleasure to be able to reassure myself that she hadn't deserted me, after all. She'd just gone for reinforcements.

I said, defending myself awkwardly, "Mac, for God's sake pull this female off me before one of these guns goes bang and kills her."

He closed the door, came forward, got a grip on the Chatham from behind, and applied some scientific leverage. I was interested to see that he knew how. One school of thought, during the war, had it that although he was great at picking, and setting up training programs for dangerous men, Mac himself couldn't fight his way out of a lightweight airmail envelope.

"All right, Miss," he said. "Behave yourself now."

Mary Frances stopped struggling in his grasp and stood there head down, panting. Her light-brown hair was a tangled cloud over her face, and there was a wide white gap between her sweater and skirt—but then, I suppose in actual life Joan of Arc went to the bonfire with stringy hair and dirty fingernails.

At the moment, I didn't care how the girl looked. She'd spoiled my Horatio-at-the-bridge act, to be sure, and made me look and feel pretty silly; but as things had turned out, it was just as well she'd interfered. I make a practice of seeing what I'm shooting at before I pull the trigger, so I probably wouldn't have fired at Mac in any case; but nevertheless, a girl who'll deliberately throw herself at two loaded guns doesn't have to comb her hair to earn my respect, no matter what her politics.

I looked from her to Mac, as he released her and stepped back. The funny thing was, he hadn't changed a bit. He was the same spare, gray man to whom I'd said goodbye in Washington, just before I picked up Beth and took off to get married. He might still have been wearing the same gray suit, for all I could tell. Oh, perhaps there was a shade more white in his close-clipped hair; perhaps the lines in his young-old face were a little more pronounced; perhaps his bleak gray eyes had retreated just a little into his skull—but they'd always been set deep beneath the dark eyebrows. I'd forgotten those eyebrows, startlingly black, seemingly immune to the aging process that had drawn the pigment from his hair. Or perhaps he dyed them for effect—there'd been some speculation about that, during the war, I remembered now, but I'd never believed it.

I said, "It's been a long time, sir."

He glanced at the guns I was holding. "Expecting trouble, Eric?"

"It seems indicated," I said. "For a moment, there, I thought you were it. Tina didn't tell me you were anywhere around."

Mac hesitated. "Well, she wasn't supposed to," he said dryly.

"I appreciate the confidence, sir," I said sourly. "There's nothing that cheers up the hired help like not knowing what the hell they're doing... Maybe, now that she's finally broken down and pried you out of hiding for me, you'll condescend to let me know what's going on."

He smiled very faintly. "Hasn't she told you?"

"Tina?" I said. "Oh, you don't have to worry your head about Tina, sir. She never lets slip unauthorized information, not even in bed. I can recommend her, without reservations, for the Noble and Exalted Order of the Clam. All I know from her is that somebody's trying to murder Amos Darrel in Santa Fe, and that we're supposed to be misleading the forces of international Communism in some vague and beautiful way by acting as sitting ducks here in San Antonio—"

I broke off. Mary Frances Chatham had raised her head, and Mac was looking at me sharply.

"Amos Darrel?" he said. "Dr. Amos Darrel? You were told he's the target in Santa Fe?"

"Why, yes," I said. "Isn't that right?"

Mac didn't answer my question. Instead, he said curtly, after a moment's pause: "I wasn't aware you'd been given that information." He glanced at the girl. "And having been given it, you should know better than to discuss it before witnesses."

I winced. "Slap my wrist, sir. I guess I've forgotten my security training."

"We'll just have to see that she has no opportunity to tell her friends how much we know."

He looked hard at the girl. Her glance dropped, and she pushed the hair out of her face and began to straighten her clothes.

I said, "Well, there are a lot of questions I want to ask, but they'd better wait. We might have visitors any minute. Where's Tina?"

"She's around," Mac said. "Never mind Tina. She's following instructions."

I said, "I'll bet. Well, I'd love to have some instructions to follow, too. I'm getting just a little tired of playing this game of yours blindfolded."

He said, "Tina wasn't explicit, there wasn't time. Just what kind of trouble are you expecting here?"

"I don't know, exactly," I said. "I don't know just what they could want with Tina and me except revenge. But they've got something fancy in mind. Somebody real tricky is running their show."

"How many agents do you figure they have available?"

"I've seen three men and one woman."

"Descriptions?"

"A young fellow, drug-store-cowboy type or a reasonable facsimile, sideburns, black hat, driving a Plymouth hardtop. An older man with a moustache, in a four-wheel-drive jeep station wagon, white and green. A Harvard-Yale-Princeton type in a golf cap, driving a blue Morris two-door, with Shorty here acting as his blushing bride. There could be more, but those are the ones who've showed."

Mac frowned thoughtfully. "It sounds as if we might be slightly outnumbered, for the moment. Arrangements are being made, but in the meantime perhaps I should have a gun, if you can spare one." He smiled that thin smile of his. "It's a long time since I've taken active part in one of these affairs, Eric. Let's see if I still remember how."

I gave him the little .38. "You hold the wooden part, sir," I said respectfully, "and pull that little metal dingus sticking out from the bottom."

He chuckled, and regarded the weapon in his hand for a moment. "This is a heavier caliber than you used to favor," he said.

"It's not mine," I said. "Spoils of war, sir. Tina got it from one of their agents—the one she had to kill."

"Ah, yes," Mac said. "The one using the alias of Herrera."

"That's right!"

He glanced at me from beneath the dark eyebrows. "So it was Tina who killed the girl? That I think, is all we needed to know."

He lifted the snubnosed revolver, and aimed it at my chest.

22

Staring at him incredulously, I heard him say, "Please drop your pistol on the bed, Eric. You won't need it any more tonight… Sarah, attend to his weapon, if you please."

I didn't have to ask who Sarah was. That would be their code name for the tall girl standing nearby—the girl I'd known as Mary Frances. Well, I'd guessed somebody clever was behind all the fancy maneuvering, but… Mac, for God's sake!

Yet, I must have suspected something, because the surprise wasn't quite paralyzing. And I suppose he could take some credit for that; he'd seen to having me well indoctrinated, at one time. I don't think any of us who went through the brutal wartime training program he set up can ever really be taken by surprise.

I was functioning again, and I looked at the little revolver with the big hole in the muzzle. And then I looked at Mac, and I grinned.

"Very neat, sir," I murmured. "But you don't really think I'd hand you a loaded gun, do you?"

I mean, it was the automatic reaction. I still was very far from comprehending what was happening and what it all meant. The simple fact was that a man was aiming a gun at me, and this, we'd had drilled into us, was a hostile act demanding instant and violent retaliation whenever possible. A man who aims a gun at you is a man who can kill you, and you don't want to leave people like that standing around. To be sure, this was a man who, two seconds earlier, I'd have said I trusted implicitly; but a gun is a gun and a threat is a threat, and I'd been trained to react first and do my heavy thinking later. And it worked.

It worked well enough that his glance dropped to the weapon for the briefest instant. It was the wrong response. There's only one answer to the old empty-gun gambit. It's the same as for the look-out-there's-somebody-behind-you routine. You just pull the damn trigger. You may wind up with a dead man on the floor, but there's a better chance of its not being you.

As he'd said, it had been a long time since he'd attended to these matters personally, and I guess he was rusty. He did look down. I still had the Colt Woodsman in my hand, muzzle down. I could have shot him, of course. That I didn't was a matter of ballistics, not sentiment—I was quite through with sentiment for the night. But a .22 doesn't pack enough punch to stop a man cold. He was holding a powerful weapon; he might still have managed to kill me, even if I'd put my little bullet squarely through his heart. I struck with the barrel instead, knocking the .38 from his hand.

His reaction was quick enough; he got my gun-wrist in some kind of a hasty lock, not a good one, but good enough that the girl had time to dart forward, grab my pistol by the barrel, and twist it backwards hard. Only the safety, still on, kept it from discharging. I had to let her take it from me; in another instant she'd have jammed and broken my finger in the trigger-guard. But Mac wasn't big enough or young enough to hold me with the incomplete grip he had. I tore myself free and reached far out and clipped the girl, as she tried to back away with the gun, sending her sprawling. The .22 jumped out of her hand and slid under the bed.

I was aware that the door had burst open, but Mac was closer and had to be attended to first. He was trying to say something. I didn't know what, or why he'd waste breath on speech at such a time. I was disappointed in him. He should have kept up on his own training system. I feinted, brushed his parry aside, and chopped him down like a tree. The girl was shouting something at me. I'd never heard such a garrulous bunch of conspirators. You'd have thought we were running a conference for radio and TV announcers instead of a fight.

Mac was at my feet, the back of his head exposed. Even without the reinforced shoes we used to wear whenever possible, one good kick would have done the job. But the girl was yelling instructions now, and other people were rushing towards us from the open door; there wasn't time to make the kill.

They were all over me as I turned. I couldn't reach the knife in my pocket. I'd spent too much time on Mac; I never got set to give them a real battle. There were too many of them; I knew they had me. There was nothing to do but grab a throat out of the melee and hang on. I used the guy as a shield in front and concentrated on squeezing the life out of him, trying to ignore the characters beating on my head and back. If I couldn't get them all—and I couldn't—I might as well do a good job on the one I had. We went down together. Presently I felt my fingers slipping. He was getting away from me, but not under his own power; and I didn't think he'd be singing in the choir next Sunday. Well, neither would I...

When I came to, I was lying on one of the room's twin beds. In the other bed, somebody was having trouble with his breathing. I can't say it bothered me. I mean, it was a matter of professional pride. I hadn't been very bright tonight. I'd been sentimental and gullible by turns, I'd let myself be licked and overpowered, but at least they couldn't say they got me free of charge. I looked up to see Mac standing over me. I didn't seem to have hurt him much. That was all right. I didn't hate him. He'd taught us that, too. He used to say that hating an enemy was a waste of time and energy. It was only necessary to kill him.

"You damn explosive lunatic!" he said softly. There was an odd, possessive note in his voice. It sounded very much like pride, although that didn't seem likely. "One forgets," he murmured. "I should have remembered that I was dealing with one of my old wartime people, instead of this new crop of pampered incompetents. I shouldn't have made the mistake of threatening you with a gun. How do you feel?"

It didn't seem like the proper time for a recital of aches and pains. "I'll probably live long enough to suit you," I whispered. "However long—or short—that may be."

He smiled. "You're soft, Eric. You should have killed me when you had me down."

"There wasn't time."

He chuckled. "You almost broke young Chatham's neck."

"My apologies for an incomplete job," I whispered. "I'll try to do better next time."

"I should be angry with you. We went through four years of war together. Do you really think I'd...?" He checked himself. "I retract the question. The mistake was mine. I shouldn't have tried to be clever with the gun. After all, you were taught to go for the throat when threatened, all of you, like savage dogs."

I whispered, "What are you trying to say, sir?"

He said, "Use your head, Eric. You're in your own room, in one of the best hotels in south Texas. There have been shouts and screams and violent blows. Where's the house detective? Where are the police?" I watched his face and said nothing. He went on: "Does it seem likely, if I'm working for the people you think, that I'd also have the full cooperation of the authorities and the hotel management?

We had the rooms on either side of you emptied, also above and below, to avoid any chance of having a guest killed by a stray bullet. That is why we closed in on you here, where we could control the surroundings. In the open, in a running fight, innocent people might have been hurt. At first we'd hoped to be able to approach you when you were alone and enlist your aid, but there was some doubt about your attitude, and anyway, you were never alone. So we laid our plans to take the two of you together. I'm glad it worked out this well. Knowing you, I was afraid we might have to kill you."

I licked my lips, still watching him closely. "Sorry to have caused you concern."

He smiled briefly, and said, "The F.B.I., as a matter of fact, isn't at all happy about your position in this matter, which is why I took the trouble of getting some statements from you on the record... Oh, yes, there's a microphone in the room." He shook his head quickly, as if reproving himself. "No, I won't pretend to be omniscient. To be perfectly honest, I wasn't quite sure where you stood myself, until I talked with you. After all, she's quite beautiful. She's made men forget their loyalties before now."

"Tina?" I whispered.

He looked down at me. "Eric, just because an attractive woman gives you a fifteen-year-old recognition signal and a plausible story...! Tina left us just three weeks after you did, right after the war. She was discharged in Paris. She's had no connection with us since. In fact, there's strong evidence to indicate that she's formed other connections... The next time somebody tries to engage you in criminal activities in my name, I wish you'd get in touch with me directly!"

"I certainly will," I said drily. "Just leave a card with your address and telephone number."

He sighed. "I suppose that's a fair criticism." He was silent briefly. Then he asked, "You believe me, don't you?"

"Oh, yes. I believe you. I guess."

I was tired, and I didn't want to think about it any more. I didn't want to think about Tina tonight. Tomorrow would be soon enough.

23

In the morning, I woke up alone in the room. There was sunlight at the window. They'd cleaned up the place. It looked tidy and innocent, like a room in which nothing had ever happened—and when you came right down to it, not much had. There'd been a little scuffle, that was all. Suspense and surprise, deceit and disillusionment, in themselves don't mark up the furniture.

The other bed was empty and neatly made up. I remembered vaguely hearing its erstwhile occupant being carted off to the hospital for some repair work on his larynx and windpipe. This should have made me feel terrible, of course—a bright and patriotic young fellow undergoing emergency surgery on my account. But as I've mentioned, we were never strong on esprit de corps. The dope should have had sense enough to keep his throat out of other people's hands; and if he'd had any training at all, he'd been taught how to break a strangle-hold, either with a smashing upward drive of both arms—hands

locked together—or finger by finger. It wasn't my fault if
he panicked and forgot his A.B.C.s.

The whole affair seemed, in retrospect, like a
remarkably stupid business; and my part in it had
certainly been no less stupid—to put it very charitably—
than anybody else's. Well, you can't be smart all the time,
but I had to admit that some people seemed to maintain a
slightly higher average than others.

There was a knock on the door, and Mac came in
without waiting for my response, followed by another
man, who closed the door and made certain it was locked
before coming forward. He gave the impression of being
a man who'd spent his life locking doors carefully before
discussing matters of vast importance. Since Mac had
said there was a mike in the room, and I had no reason to
believe it had been removed, I wasn't too impressed by
this concern for locks and doors.

The man was, I judged, a well-preserved fifty, with the
rangy, powerful build of a college football star who'd put
on a little middle-aged weight and would have put on more
if it hadn't been for the rowing machine and the handball
court. His face had a hint of Lincolnesque angularity, of
which he was aware. It was the only angularity about
him. In all other respects he was a real smoothie.

I was interested to see that he was carrying Tina's
handsome fur piece carefully folded. He held it gingerly,
with a hint of dramatized embarrassment, the way
some men handle anything recognizably feminine, as
if they want to make damn sure you understand they're

not in the habit of fondling items of this kind and get no kick from it. You see them in the dress shops around December, putting on an act as if they thought the black lace Christmas lingerie would bite them.

I glanced at the mink stole as he laid it on the foot of the bed. It was a clue, no doubt, but I didn't try to interpret it. It could have been taken off her body—alive or dead—or she could have dropped it as she made good her escape. And why had it been brought here and planted conspicuously on my bedclothes? That too, would become clear in due time. It was nothing worth wasting cerebral energy on until I knew more about it.

I looked at Mac and said, "How many keys are there to this trap, anyway? I might as well have put up a cot in a public john."

Mac said, "I brought Mr. Denison to see you. Show him your credentials, Denison, to make it official."

The latter-day Lincoln showed me some credentials that had impressive words on them, although I suppose he could have got them with a box of Cracker-Jacks.

I said, "Fine. He's seen me and I've seen him. What do we do now?"

"He wants to ask you some questions," Mac said. "Answer to the best of your ability, Eric. There's full cooperation between Mr. Denison's organization and ours."

I liked that little word "ours." It meant I was back in the fold, at least for the time being.

"Full?" I asked.

"Full."

"Okay," I said. "What do you want to know, Mr. Denison?"

As might have teen expected, he wanted the whole story, and I gave it to him. He didn't believe a word of it. Oh, I don't mean he thought I was lying. But he didn't think I was telling the truth, either. He didn't think anything about it, one way or the other. He was just collecting spoken words from one M. Helm, as a doctor might have collected specimens of my blood and urine.

"Ah, well, it looks like we've got most of it," he said at last. "You say—" He referred to some notes he'd taken. "—you say this woman at one point showed you a membership card in a certain subversive organization?"

"Yes. She claimed to have found it among the dead girl's effects."

"It was probably her own. You don't happen to recall the number of the card?"

"No," I said. "The code name was Dolores."

"If you'd examined the physical description of the holder with reasonable care, Mr. Helm, I think you'd have discovered it couldn't very well have applied to Miss Herrera."

"Perhaps," I said. "They were both dark-haired girls of about the same height. The eyes were different, of course." I found myself wondering, quite irrelevantly, just how some hardboiled party official had gone about describing the color of Tina's eyes.

"And you say the body is hidden in the old Santander mine?"

"That's right. Check with Carlos Juhan in Cerrillos, he'll tell you how to get in there. You'll have an easier job if you take a jeep or four-wheel-drive pickup."

"It seems to me…" Denison hesitated.

"Yes?"

"It seems to me you lent yourself to this scheme without much thought. I can't quite understand how a reputable citizen, with a wife and three small children, could allow himself to be persuaded—"

Mac spoke up abruptly. "I'll take it from here, Denison. Thanks a lot for coming up."

"Yes," Denison said. "Ah, yes. Of course."

He went out, rather stiffly. Mac followed him to the door, and locked it behind him; then strode to a picture on the nearby wall, took a microphone out from behind it, and pulled out the cord by the roots. He tossed the mike into the wastebasket, and turned to look at me.

"You don't know how lucky you are, Eric," he said.

I glanced at the door through which Denison had gone. "I can guess. He'd love to see me in jail."

Mac shook his head. "I wasn't referring to that, although it's a point." He came to the foot of the bed, and reached down to stroke the soft fur of Tina's mink stole, without embarrassment. "She got away," he said. "She hid in the hotel, trying to wait us out, but they caught her outside. They got her gun and made her clasp her hands at the back of her neck, but it seems there was a little throwing knife…"

"I didn't know she had that. She must have taken it

off the body when I wasn't looking." I grimaced. "I bet she didn't hurt anybody much. She never was much good with a knife."

"Well, one of Denison's men is having some stitches taken in his face, but I suppose you could say he wasn't seriously hurt. The other one just got this fur wrapped around his head. By the time he could see again, she was gone. So I guess you could call it a draw, this time. She got away, but at least you're alive to tell us about it."

I looked at him for a little. He did not speak. I asked the question he was waiting for. "What do you mean," I said, "this time?"

"Oh," he said, "she's used the same technique before, pretending to be carrying out my orders. But the other suckers were dead when she left them." He looked at me for a moment. "She's been looking up all our old people, Eric, the ones she worked with during the war. It's surprising how many of them seem to be ripe for a little excitement, even the settled ones with families. When I recognized the pattern, I sent operatives to warn all her likely prospects—but Herrera didn't reach you quite in time." After a little silence, he said, "She must be found and stopped, Eric. She has done enough harm. I want you to find her and stop her. Permanently."

24

When I paid my hotel bill, the woman at the cashier's window smiled pleasantly and said, "You come back, Mr. Helm."

I didn't know why she'd want me back, after last night's ruckus, and she probably didn't know herself, but the phrase has become almost obligatory for employees of business institutions throughout the southwest. Whether you drop in five times a day or don't ever expect to see the place again, you're always told to come back.

Driving north from San Antonio, there's the usual freeway routine—at least, they called them freeways out in California when I was there. Maybe the Texans have another name for them. Driving was a cinch, and I had plenty of time to think. My thinking revolved mainly around Mac's expression when I told him to go to hell. At that point, he'd stopped being his new, sociable, smiling, peacetime self. Well, I hadn't put much stock in that act, anyway.

There wasn't really much he could do about it, short of calling in Denison and having me arrested for something, which apparently didn't appeal to him. Instead, he'd told me how to get in touch with him, if I should change my mind, and stalked out, leaving the mink stole lying on the foot of my bed. It was in the back of the pickup now, as I drove north along the four-lane highway that, as near as I could figure out, more or less followed the route of the old Shawnee Trail to Kansas. So I wasn't rid of her entirely, and if you think that wasn't Mac's idea in leaving it, you don't know Mac. He'd saddled me with something of hers he was reasonably sure I wouldn't sell, burn, or give away. There was only one way for me to get rid of it; and while it was a long chance—after all, I had no idea where she'd gone, and he probably knew it—I was sure that if it should happen, he or some of his people wouldn't be very far away.

Well, that was his worry, or maybe it was Tina's. If she wanted her furs, she could come and get them. If he wanted her, he could come and get her. I wasn't going to play delivery boy or bird dog for either of them. I'd had my little fling at reviving my old, tough, wartime self, and the experiment hadn't been a howling success. I was going back to being a peaceful writer looking for material, a devoted father and a faithful husband—although the last might take some doing, after what had happened.

I got off the concrete and went down the little back roads from which I could see and feel the country, zigzagging northwards. I slept in the truck that night. It rained hard the next day. If anybody was following me in anything but a jeep, he had lots of fun. In places, it was all the truck could do to make it through the gluey gumbo, for all its cleated tires and four-speed transmission. I didn't mind. The nice thing about driving a truck is, you don't have to worry about the wheels falling off just because the road doesn't happen to be perfectly smooth and dry.

I crossed the rivers with the great ringing names out of Western history: the Trinity, the Colorado, the Brazos, and the Red. The weather cleared, and I shot Kodachrome by the yard. I went on north through Oklahoma and into the southeast corner of Kansas. They found lead and zinc in that corner of the state around the turn of the century, and they dug up the whole country and stacked it in great gray piles behind the mine structures, now mostly abandoned and falling into decay. It makes a weird-looking landscape, and creates difficulties for a writer trying to figure out what the place looked like before the digging.

I began working my way westwards, having completed my main chore. I could have gone straight home, I suppose, but the fact is, I still wasn't quite sure I was going home. And if I did go home, I had no idea what to say to Beth when I got there. I suppose you could say I was stalling while I tried to think up some excuses for my inexcusable behavior. Anyway, it seemed a pity to come so close to the old roaring cattle towns of Abilene, Ellsworth, Hays, and Dodge City without stopping to see what they looked like.

Abilene was a waste of time. They had no sense of their historical past; they were much prouder of President Eisenhower, it seemed, than of Wild Bill Hickok. As a writer of Western stories, I found this hard to understand. Ellsworth was just a sleepy little prairie town on a big railroad. Hays I didn't get to because daylight was running out on me, and it would have taken me too far northwards, anyway. I kept plugging to the south and west and hit Dodge City shortly after dark. It was time for a bath and a night in a real bed, so I pulled into the first tourist court that looked passable, cleaned up, and went into town to eat. Here they'd gone to the other extreme: the whole place was a museum of the old cowboy days. I cruised back and forth along the dark streets for a while, kind of lining up the places I wanted to see when they opened in the morning.

When I got back to my room at the tourist court, the phone was ringing. I knew nobody in this town, and I'd told nobody I was coming here, but the phone was ringing. I closed the door gently behind me, and walked over and picked it up.

"Mr. Helm?" It was the voice of the motel manager. "I just happened to see you drive in. You have a long-distance call from Santa Fe, New Mexico. Just a minute."

I sat down on the bed and waited. I heard him get the operator, and I heard the phone ring five hundred miles away, and I heard Beth answer. The sound of her voice made me feel guilty and ashamed of myself. I could at least have called her from San Antonio, as I'd promised to do. But I'd sent a couple of cards to the boys. You don't have to say anything on a picture postcard.

"Matt?"

"Yes," I said.

"Matt," she said, speaking in a tight, breathless way, "Matt, Betsy's gone! She disappeared from her playpen on the front porch an hour ago, while I was making dinner… And before I could notify the police, that man who was at the Darrels' party, the big, mean-looking one, Loris, called up and said she would be safe if—" Beth hesitated.

"If what?"

"If you were willing to cooperate. He said to tell you… to tell you somebody was waiting to see you with a proposition. He said you'd know who he meant… Oh, Matt, what is it, what's going on?"

25

After I'd hung up the phone, I sat for a little while looking at the silent instrument. I suppose I was thinking, but there wasn't, when you came right down to it, a great deal to think about. The next move was obvious. Loris had given Beth full instructions: not only what to tell me, but also where to reach me. To know this, the way I'd been moving around the past few days, he had to have a man following me. This man would undoubtedly be standing by right now to see how I reacted to my wife's phone call.

My orders were to head for home, where further instructions would be waiting by the time I arrived. There wasn't much choice. They'd be waiting for their boy's report. I couldn't even make any useful calls; he might be listening in, somehow. I had to be seen driving off obediently in the right direction, so that he could get on the phone and let them know that the first stage had fired properly and the projectile seemed to be headed towards a satisfactory orbit.

I got up and packed my things quickly, loaded them into the rear of the pickup, and climbed into the cab. There was a certain amount of suspense as I drove through the town; I couldn't tell whether or not I was being followed. But he was a thorough workman, and I picked him up in the rearview mirrors shortly after we left the city limits. I could hardly miss him. He was driving a new car with one of those four-lamp setups that ought to be banned. They have two beam levels; one merely blinds you temporarily, but the other's a lulu, capable of incinerating the retina and searing the optic nerve if the guy doesn't dim in time, which he generally doesn't, particularly if he's coming up from behind.

This chap was a real mirror-burner-upper. My problem wasn't keeping track of him, it was staying on the road with all four of his searchlights glaring at me from two mirrors. I guess he felt it was his turn to crow: I must have given him a hard run across three states—he may even have thought I'd done it deliberately—and now he was damn well going to escort me on my way in style.

He stuck with me through the first small town west of Dodge; then, suddenly, he was gone. I kept on driving, knowing he'd have to give me at least one chance to pull a fast one before he made his report, or his conscience wouldn't let him sleep. It was a long fifteen minutes; then a car doing at least eighty-five came up from behind and whipped past and went on to the west down that long straight road. It was a new white Chevy.

I wasn't sure this was my man, but he was waiting for

me up the highway, and fell in step behind me when I passed. We proceeded in this way for another half dozen miles, then he disappeared from my mirrors, and I looked back in time to see him swinging into a roadside joint I'd just passed. I gave him a little time, and turned back, stopping well before I reached the place. I went ahead on foot. The lights were on, and the white fan-tail Chevy was parked by the building with half a dozen other cars. It was empty; my man was apparently inside.

I had a long wait. I guess, his duty done, his report made, he'd taken time for a coffee and a piece of pie. It probably wasn't a drink, since Kansas has some legislation on that subject, too. At last he came out. I was behind him as he paused by the car door to find his keys. He was a pro; he didn't move when the barrel of the Woodsman touched him in the back.

"Helm?" he said after a moment.

"That's right."

"You're a fool. I've just talked to a certain party in Santa Fe. Any tricks you pull will come out of your little girl's—"

The safety of the gun made a soft snicking sound in the darkness, cutting him short. I said gently, "Don't remind me of things like that, little man. It's very hard on my self-control. My truck's right down the road. Let's go."

I kept him covered while he drove. It was only nine thirty when we pulled up in front on my cabin at the Dodge City tourist court, although it seemed much later. I hated to back-track so far, but it was the only place I could take him without attracting attention, and I needed a temporary headquarters with a phone.

"Lift up the seat," I said after we'd got down from the cab. "There's a roll of wire and a pair of pliers underneath."

He was really a small man, I saw, when I got light on him at last, inside the room with the door closed—a small, shabby, inconspicuous man in a brown suit. He had brown eyes, too. They looked shiny and glassy, like cheap brown marbles. I wired his hands behind him and then I wired his ankles together. He didn't have a gun. I sat down by the phone and made a long distance call. Mac answered right away. It was as though he'd been expecting to hear from me.

I said, "Eric here. The Paradise Cafe, ten miles west of Cimarron, Kansas. A long distance call to Santa Fe, New Mexico, made just before nine o'clock, to what number? When you find out, have the place covered, and call me back."

I gave him the number of my telephone, and hung up. The little man was watching me with expressionless brown eyes.

I said, "You'd better hope he can trace the call. Otherwise, it's up to you."

He laughed scornfully. "You think I'd tell you, mister?"

I took the Solingen from my pocket and started cleaning my fingernails with the long blade. They didn't need cleaning, but it's always an effective menace bit, if not exactly original.

"I think you would," I said without looking up.

He stopped laughing. We waited in silence. After a while I got a magazine and lay down on the bed to read. I won't pretend the stuff made a great deal of sense. It seemed a hell of a long time before the telephone rang. I picked it up.

"Eric speaking."

Mac's voice said, "The call went to Hotel DeCastro, Santa Fe. Mr. Fred Loring."

"That would be Frank Loris?"

"The description fits."

"Is Mr. Loring alone, or does he have a wife and baby daughter with him? Or maybe just a baby daughter?"

Mac didn't answer at once. Then he said, "That's the play, is it?"

"That's the play," I said.

"What's your answer going to be?"

"I called you, didn't I?" I said.

"Do we have a deal?"

"Yes," I said. There was no choice now. I had to have his help. "Yes, we have a deal."

"You know what I want? You'll make the touch?"

I said, "Don't push it. I know what you want. I'll make the touch. Now, is Loris alone?"

"Yes," Mac said. "He's alone."

I drew a long breath. Well, I hadn't expected it would be that easy. I said, "You've got him covered? I want to be able to put my hand on him any time of the day or night I get there and ask for him."

"He's covered," Mac said. "You'll get him. But

remember, it isn't Loris I'm interested in."

I ignored this. "Also," I said, "you'd better send somebody over here with a badge to impress the motel manager. If he's listening at his switchboard, he's apt to be getting nervous. Then there's a white '59 Chevy parked in front of that cafe I mentioned. If you don't want questions asked, better take care of it. Finally, there's the driver of the Chevy. I've got him here with me. Send somebody over here who can be trusted to keep him away from a phone. He's reported me on my way; I don't want him confusing them with any more calls."

Mac said, "Fortunately, we've been keeping a casual eye on you—from a distance—after we discovered you were being followed by somebody else. One of our people is in Dodge City now. I can have him over there in ten minutes."

"One more thing," I said. "I want a fast car. You don't happen to have a stray Jag or Corvette handy?"

Mac laughed. "I'm afraid not, but the man I'm sending over has a fairly fast little Plymouth. I'm told it'll do a hundred and thirty, which should be adequate."

I groaned. "That finned monster I saw down in Texas? Well, okay, if that's the best you can do."

Mac said, "Don't kill yourself on the road. Eric—"

"Yes?"

"We didn't really expect them to have the nerve to return to Santa Fe. We were looking for them elsewhere. Did Loris happen to say what they wanted from you?"

"I didn't talk to him personally," I said. "My wife

took the message. But he apparently didn't say anything except that they had the baby and a proposition for me."

"I see." Mac hesitated. Probably he had in mind saying something about how much he trusted me, how greatly he relied upon me to do the right thing, and how deeply grieved he'd be if I should let him down. If so, he strangled the impulse, which was just as well. He said crisply, "All right. When you get to Santa Fe, call this number."

He gave me the number. I wrote it down, and hung up the phone. Then I looked at the man in the brown suit, sitting on the floor in the corner.

He said defiantly, "I'm not worrying a bit, mister. Loris will take you without raising a sweat."

"Loris?" I said. I grinned at him, not very nicely. "Let's not talk about the walking dead, little man."

He looked at me for a moment longer, and started to speak again, but changed his mind. Presently there was a knock at the door. I took my pistol and went to open it, taking the usual precautions. They weren't necessary. It was the kid of the black hat and the sideburns who'd been driving the Plymouth when I saw it last, except that he'd changed his disguise. Now he looked like a college boy. It was a definite improvement, but, then, just about any change would have been.

"Watch that heap," he said. "She looks corny, but she's a ball of fire."

I jerked my head towards the bound man. "See he doesn't get to a phone," I said. "And if you want to drive my truck, here's the key. Use a light foot. That's not a racing mill under the hood, so don't tear it up."

He said, "You've got everything except brakes. They haven't invented those yet in Detroit. Keep it in mind going through the mountains."

I nodded, and went over to get my suitcase out of the rear of the pickup. He went in to his prisoner. We didn't say goodbye.

26

I put two pounds more air in the tires all around while the attendant was filling the tank. Then I walked twice around the car to stretch my legs, regarding my borrowed vehicle with awe and wonder. It was the ugliest damn hunk of automotive machinery I'd ever had the misfortune to be associated with, not barring even Beth's glamorized station wagon. It had a great bubble of a windshield obviously designed to make the front seat uninhabitable any time the sun was shining. A nice commentary on these wheeled greenhouses is the number of them you see on our Western roads with roadmaps, magazines, towels, anything, held up against all that glass to keep the passengers from being broiled alive. There was a kind of potty-seat on the rear deck between the fins. It must have been that, because it had nothing to do with the spare tire. I looked. All it needed, obviously, was to be hooked up to a little plumbing, and you'd be all set for the times Junior couldn't hold out until the next restroom.

"That'll be three-forty, Mister," the filling station attendant said. "Oil and water okay. That's quite a car you've got there. I tell you, I don't get it, folks buying these lousy-looking little foreign cars when they can get something real sharp made right here in America."

Well, it's all a matter of taste, I guess. I paid him, got in, remembered that the key worked the starter for some unexplained reason, and that the right-hand row of push-buttons had something to do with the heater; it was the left-hand row that ran the car. The idea of having to locate a certain little white button on the dashboard when you want second gear seems fairly idiotic to me, but obviously I'm not in tune with the times. There were all kinds of colored lights in front of me, but no ammeter or oil-pressure gauge. I didn't even think about a tachometer. Why dream? I turned the key, pushed button number one, stepped on the accelerator, and the machine took off.

I still didn't have quite the feel of it, so there was a certain amount of sliding and screeching before we got straightened out on the highway. By this time the speedometer needle was coming up to forty-five, and I reached out and socked button number two. There was a gadget somewhere around that would do the shifting for me, but I'm peculiar, I like to pick my own gears. This one took me up to eighty, and even so the beast was loafing. I hit number three and we went up past a hundred with a rush; and now you could hear, above the sound of the wind, the sighing roar of the two big four-barrel carburetors reaching for air.

I mean, it was a lot of car. Not only did it have the power—everybody's got power these days—but it was steady as a rock. Underneath all the weird styling dreamed up by the butterfly boys, some real engineers had got together and concocted something quite commendable. I let my mind toy with the possibility of getting Beth to trade in the Buick; maybe I could get this car with a stick shift if I held a gun on somebody…

I let my mind wander like this as I drove. I didn't need time to think. I'd done all the necessary thinking. I knew what had to be done. All I needed was to keep from thinking, now, until the time came to do it.

It was two hundred miles, give or take a few, to La Junta, Colorado, pronounced La Hunta. I was well ahead of schedule by that time, so I found a place that was open and put down a cup. of coffee and a piece of soggy apple pie. Then I swung southwest towards Trinidad and Raton. I was kind of sorry to be coming this way in the dark. There's always a fine moment of excitement when you first raise the snowcapped peaks of the Rockies over the edge of the plains ahead, on any road. You can even imagine, if you try hard, something of what the sight must have meant to the early pioneers after a couple of months on the trail.

I didn't think about Betsy, and I didn't think about Beth, or Loris, or Tina, or Mac. I just pushed the car along and listened to the roar of the engine and the howl of the wind and the whine of the tires, holding her as close to a hundred as the road would allow, which was usually pretty close in the flat country. Beyond Trinidad, however, the road headed up into the mountains towards Raton Pass and my home state of New Mexico. Going up was no problem with all that power; coming down again on the other side was a slightly different matter, involving, as it did, some hard use of the brakes. They got fairly hot and feeble before we got down off that hill. I didn't dare do any trick braking with the funny push-button transmission, not knowing how much, or little, it could take. Besides, it had its own ideas about when to shift, and they weren't mine.

Out on the flat again, the smell of burned brake lining gradually blew away. At the junction south of the town of Raton, I took the left-hand fork towards Las Vegas. Yes, we've got a town in New Mexico by that name, too. In Las Vegas, I found another cup of coffee and a couple of fried eggs with bacon. Some time after that, the sky started to get light in the east, which was all right. In the truck, I'd have been coming in around ten in the morning. I'd told Beth to expect me about that time. This way, I'd actually hit town around six, which would give me plenty of time for the arrangements I had to make.

Figuring like this, confidently, I almost piled up in Glorieta Pass, not fifty miles from home. Coming up to a curve too fast, I suddenly discovered I had no more brakes than a roller skate. An ordinary car would have rolled and wound up at the bottom of the canyon, but this one kept right side up as I took the corner in a screaming slide, using the whole road. It would have been a hell of a time to meet somebody coming the other way. After that, as long as I was in the hills, I kept the transmission locked in second gear, used the compression judiciously to slow her down, and took it much easier. There wasn't that much of a hurry, anyway.

I made my entrance into town by way of a small dirt road instead of the main highway, just in case somebody might be watching for me. The first filling station I hit was closed, but it had a public phone booth outside. I stopped the car—the brakes had recovered enough for casual use—got out stiffly, and made my call to the number Mac had given me.

When somebody answered, I said, "This is the Dodge City, Santa Fe Express, coming in on Track Three."

"Who?" the guy said. Some people have no sense of humor. "Mr. Helm?"

"Yes, this is Helm."

"Your subject is still in his room at the DeCastro Hotel," the guy said. He had a clipped, businesslike, Eastern voice. "He has company. Female."

"Who?"

"Nobody we're interested in. Just someone he picked up in the bar. What are your plans?"

"I'll be sitting in the lobby when he comes down," I said.

"Is that wise?"

"It remains to be seen," I said. "Don't call off the watchdogs. He might try to backdoor me."

"I'll be over there myself," the voice said. "There'll be

a man standing phone watch at this number, however, in case you want to get in touch with us again. He'll be able to relay any messages to me."

"Very good," I said. "Thanks." I hung up, found another dime, and dialed again. There was only a little pause before Beth answered. If she'd been sleeping at all, it wasn't soundly. "Good morning," I said.

"Matt! Where are you?"

"I'm in Raton," I said. After all, there might be somebody on the line. "Ran into a little trouble in the mountains. The truck threw a connecting rod—I guess I was pushing too hard. But I've managed to wake up a guy who'll rent me a bar, and I'll be on my way as soon as I hang up." That would explain the Plymouth, if anybody was watching when I drove up. It would also explain any delays, if I ran into trouble. I asked, "Any news? Any further instructions for me?"

"Not yet."

"Get any sleep?"

"Not much," she said. "How could I?"

"That makes two of us," I said. "Okay. When somebody calls, tell her I may be just a little late, and explain why."

"Her?" Beth said.

"It'll be a her, this time," I said, hoping I was right.

27

She was a Spanish-American girl, dark and willing-looking, but a little past the prettiest time of her life, which comes early among that race. She was wearing one of those small gray jackets made of nylon fur, over a yellow sweater and a tight gray skirt tricked out around the bottom with a lot of little pleats. Somehow, whenever one of those girls gets hold of a narrow skirt, which isn't often, it's always several inches too long; and the tartier the girl, strangely enough, the longer the skirt. You'd think it would be the other way around.

This one was pretty well hobbled. She came across the hotel lobby in her high heels and went out into the morning sunlight. Presently a man came in to buy a paper at the cigar counter. His crisp Eastern voice was familiar; I'd heard it over the phone quite recently. He walked on past me towards the coffee shop, a moderately tall character, well set up, in a gray suit—too young, handsome, and clean-cut for my taste, the epitome of a modern law-enforcement officer, no doubt, with good training in law or accounting as well as marksmanship and judo. He could have taken me with either hand, while lighting a cigarette with the other; but he'd never get the chance; he was too nice a boy. I was going to have trouble with him. I could smell it.

He didn't look at me as he went past, but his head kind of bobbed in a nod, to tell me it was the right girl and things might start to happen, now that she was out of the way. It was about time. I'd been sitting there for an hour and a half.

He'd hardly gone out of sight when Loris appeared at the head of the short flight of stairs that led to the rear of the hotel, whatever might be there. He was yawning. He needed a shave, but with my beard I was hardly in a position to criticize. I'd forgotten how big he was. He looked tremendously solid, standing there above me, and handsome in a bull-like way. The place was lousy with handsome young men. I felt old as the Sangre de Cristo peaks above the town, ugly as an adobe wall, and mean as a prairie rattlesnake. I'd driven four hundred miles in the truck since yesterday morning and five hundred miles in the Plymouth since last night, but it didn't matter. Weariness just served to anesthetize my conscience, if I had one, which wasn't likely. Mac had done his best to amputate it long ago. It was, he said, a handicap in our line of business.

Loris looked down and saw me. He wasn't very good. His eyes widened with recognition, and he glanced quickly towards the phone booths in the corner. Obviously his first impulse was to report this development and ask for advice.

I shook my head minutely, and made a slight gesture towards the street. Then I picked up the magazine I'd been pretending to read for an hour and a half, but I was aware that it took him several seconds to start moving again. He wasn't a lightning brain, by a long shot. I was counting on that.

He came down the steps and walked past me, hesitated, and went on out the front door. I got up casually and followed him. He was kind of shuffling his feet outside, moving off to the left slowly while waiting to see if I was coming. Now that I was here, he didn't want to lose me, even if he didn't quite know what to do with me. I wasn't supposed to be here this early.

He kept going, looking back to see that I was following, moving in the direction of the Santa Fe River, at this time of year a small trickle of water running over sand and rocks between high hanks; in places the banks were reinforced by stone floodwalls. I've seen times when it came over the banks and walls and caused considerable local excitement. Along the river was a narrow green park with grass and trees and picnic tables; and the streets of the town went over the stream on low, arched bridges, like giant culverts. Loris got to the park and headed upstream, cutting across the grass, past the picnic tables, obviously looking for a place where we could have a little privacy. He wanted enough privacy, I guessed, to be able to knock me around a bit, if necessary. It would be what came naturally into his mind.

I followed him, keeping my eyes on his broad back, hating him. I could afford to hate him now. There was no longer any need for calmness and clear thinking. I'd flushed him out of cover, I had him in the open, and I could think of Betsy, and of Beth waiting at home without sleep. I could even think, if I wanted to be petty, of a poke I'd once taken in the solar plexus, of a crack across the neck and a kick in the ribs. I could add up the balance sheet on Mr. Frank Loris and find, not much to my surprise, that there wasn't any really good reason for the guy to keep on living.

He picked the spot as well as I could have picked it myself, in broad daylight with the town coming awake around us and all the law-abiding citizens hurrying off to their law-abiding jobs. He ducked down the bank, jumped from rock to rock down there, and vanished under a bridge. I slid down after him.

It was medium dark under the bridge. We had a wide street with sidewalks above us, and in the center the light had quite a ways to travel from the half-moon-shaped openings at either end. The river made a little trickle of sound to my right as I walked towards him. He'd stopped to wait for me. As I came up, he was saying something. His attitude was impatient and bullying. I suppose he was asking what the hell I was doing there, and telling me what would happen to me or to Betsy if I was trying to pull something…

I didn't hear the words, maybe because of the sound of the river, maybe because I simply wasn't listening. There was nothing he had to say that I had to hear. There were a couple of cars going past overhead. It was as good a time as any. I took out the gun and shot him five times in the chest.

28

It could have been done more neatly, but they were small bullets and he was a big man and I wanted to be sure. He looked very surprised—so surprised that he never moved at all in the time it took me to empty half a ten-shot clip. There was a gun of some kind under his armpit; I could see the bulge of it through his coat. He never reached for it. He was a muscle man. They can seldom be trained to think in terms of weapons. He put down his head and charged, reaching for me with his big hands. I sidestepped and tripped him.

He went down and didn't get up again. The wheezy breath from his punctured lungs wasn't very pleasant to listen to. If he'd been a deer, I'd have put a quick one into his neck to cut it short, but you're not supposed to dispense that kind of mercy to human beings. Anyway, I didn't want the body to display any bullet-holes in the wrong places. Mac would want a reasonable story to give to the newspapers.

Loris collapsed and rolled over on his side. I reached down and took the revolver from under his armpit. It was a huge weapon, just the sort of hand cannon I'd expected him to lug around and then forget completely when he might have some use for it. It was wet with his blood. I carried it to the bridge opening, and stepped back quickly as I heard someone come running and sliding down the rocks towards me.

It was the Boy Scout in the gray suit. He charged in with drawn, short-barreled revolver in his hand. I suppose it took courage, and maybe that's the way you have to do it when you wear a badge and think a citizen's life may be at stake, but it seemed reckless and impractical to me.

"Drop it," I said from the shadows.

He started to turn, but checked himself. "Helm?"

"Drop it," I said. He'd be the kind to get excited and officious at the sight of a body full of bullet-holes.

"But—"

"Mister," I said softly, "drop it. I won't tell you again." I was beginning to shake just a little. Maybe it showed in my voice. The revolver dropped into the sand. I said, "Now step away from it." He did as he was told. I said, "Now turn around."

He turned and looked at me. "What the hell's got into you? I thought I heard shots—" A harsh, rattling sound made him look upstream. Apparently Loris was still alive. The guy in the gray suit looked that way, shocked. "Why," he said, "you crazy fool—"

I asked, "What were your instructions concerning me?"

"I was told to give you all the assistance—"

"Calling me names doesn't assist me much," I said.

"You used us to finger the man!" he protested. "To point him out to you, so you could deliberately shoot him down!"

"What did you think I was going to do, kiss him on the cheek?"

He said, stiffly, "I realize how you must feel, Mr. Helm, with your little girl missing, but this kind of private justice—"

I said, "You're the only one talking about justice."

"Anyway, alive he might have led us to—"

"He'd have led us nowhere useful," I said. "He was dumb, but not that dumb. And he couldn't have been made to talk. Men like that have no imagination and no nervous system to work on. But he could, if something went wrong, have got to Betsy and harmed her. It's the only way he'd have led us to her, and we'd have had to wait until the last minute to make sure he was going to the right place. We might not have been able to stop him in time. Given a chance—and you'd have insisted on giving him a chance—he could have been a hard man to stop. I can do better with him out of the way." I glanced upstream. "I suppose you'll want to call an ambulance, since he's still breathing. Tell the doctor to be real careful. We wouldn't want him to live."

The young man in the gray suit looked distressed at my callousness. "Mr. Helm, you simply cannot take the law into your own hands."

I looked at him for a moment, and he shut up. "What's your name?" I asked.

"Bob Calhoun."

I said, "Mr. Calhoun, I want you to listen to me very closely. I'm trying to be a rational man of sound judgment. I'm trying very hard. But my little girl is in danger, and so help me God, if you get in my way with your damn fool scruples and legalisms, I'll swat you like a mosquito… Now this is what I want you to do. I want you to go back to that office of yours and keep that phone clear. I don't care who calls; get him off the line fast. If you've got to go to the john, have them bring a pot into the room for you. I'll be wanting you quick some time in the next couple of hours, and I don't want to have to stand around waiting for them to run you down with bloodhounds. Do I make myself clear, Mr. Calhoun?"

He said angrily, "Listen, Helm—"

I said, "You have your orders. You're supposed to assist me. Well, don't think about it, just do it. I can assure you that higher echelons will spray it all with perfume and tie it up with a pink ribbon, once it's over." I drew a long breath. "Keep that wire clear, Calhoun. And while you're waiting, get a crew of good men ready to move fast. Set up all the local cooperation you're going to need to wrap up a whole city block the minute I give you the address. You boys are supposed to be good at that stuff. It's out of my line; I'm leaving it to you. I'm counting on you to get my kid out safely, once I tell you where she is."

He said, "Very well. We'll do our best." His voice

was stiff and reluctant, but politer than it had been. He hesitated and said, "Mr. Helm?"

"Yes?"

"If you don't mind my asking," he said, "just what is your line?"

I glanced towards Loris, who was still breathing a little. You had to hand it to the guy, he was tough as a buffalo. But I didn't think he'd last much longer.

"Why," I said gently, "killing's my line, Mr. Calhoun." I turned and left the two of them there.

It seemed very odd to be coming home, like any businessman returning from a trip. I parked in the drive. The door burst open, and Beth came running towards me and stumbled into my arms. I held her kind of gingerly. If you feel a certain way about a woman, and your work involves, say, a garbage truck or a butcher shop, you like to clean up a bit before you put your hands on her. I couldn't help feeling I must stink of blood and gun powder, not to mention another woman.

"Any messages?" I asked after a little.

"Yes," she breathed, as if in answer to my thought. "A woman called. And… and there was something else…"

"What?"

"Something… something horrible…"

I drew a long breath. "Show me," I said.

She led me onto the porch. "She… told me over the phone to look out here. I don't know how long it had been here when she called, I didn't hear anybody… She said it was to… to change your mind, in case you were trying to be… clever…"

It was a shoe box, tucked back in a corner behind one of our porch chairs, I suppose so the older kids wouldn't find and investigate it on their way to school. I pushed it out into the open with my foot, and looked at the box, and at my wife. Her face was white. I bent down and untied the string and opened the box. Our gray tomcat was inside, quite dead and rather messily disemboweled.

The funny thing was, it made me mad. It could have been so much worse; yet instead of feeling relieved, I was grieved and angry, remembering the fun the kids had had with the poor stupid beast, and all the mornings it had been at the kitchen door to greet me, meowing for its milk… I remembered also that this cat had once scared hell out of Tina by stowing away in the truck with her. She wasn't one to forget small injuries, if she could pay them back conveniently. Well, neither was I.

"Cover it up, please!" Beth said in a choked voice. "Poor Tiger! Matt, what kind of person would… would do something like that?"

I put the lid back on the box and straightened up. I wanted to tell her: *a person very much like me.* It was a message from Tina to me. She was saying that the fun was over and from now on everything was strictly business and I could expect no concessions from her on the grounds of sentiment. Well, I had a message for her, too. And while I'm moderately fond of animals, and capable of feeling grief for a family pet, I can take an awful lot of dead cats if I have to.

"What are my instructions?" I asked.

Beth said, "Take… *it* out back. I'll get a shovel. It's Mrs. Garcia's day to clean the house. I'll tell you out there."

I nodded and picked up the box, carried it into the back yard, and set it down near the softest looking spot in the flowerbed at the side of the studio. It occurred to me that I was practically making a career of disposing of bodies, human and animal. Beth joined me. I took the shovel and started to dig.

She said, "At ten o'clock, or as soon afterwards as you get here, you're supposed to drive out to Cerrillos Road. There's a motel just outside the city limits on the right-hand side, a kind of truck stop with a gas station and restaurant—you remember the one, with shabby little cabins in back, red and white. Tony's Place. You're to go to the cabin farthest from the road. But don't park there. First leave your car where everybody else does, by the restaurant. And if anybody follows you, or anything happens, Betsy—"

"All right, no need to spell it out," I said as she hesitated. I stuck the box into the hole I'd made and covered it up. I looked at my watch. "Check my time," I said. "A quarter of ten."

"I have ten of ten," she said, "but I'm just a little fast. Matt—"

"What?"

"She called you Eric once, by mistake. Why? She sounded as if… as if she knew you quite well. At the Darrels' party you said you'd never seen her before."

"That's right," I said. "I did say that, but it wasn't the truth. Beth…"

I patted the dirt into place over Tiger's grave, and straightened up—leaning on the long-handled shovel—and looked at her. Her light-brown hair was a little rumpled, as if she hadn't spent much time on it this morning, but it looked soft and bright in the sunshine. She was wearing a loose green sweater and a green plaid skirt, and she looked very young, like the college girl I'd married when I'd had no business marrying anyone—young, and tired, and scared, and pretty, and innocent.

It was time for me to remember the standing orders. *Look her in the eye and lie*, Mac had said that day in Washington, *lie and keep on lying…* Never mind exactly what I told her. It was the kind of stuff I put on paper and sell for money. It seemed that, like many other Americans overseas, I'd become involved with a black-market ring while I was stationed in London. Now some of the members had suddenly reappeared in my life with a crooked proposition which I'd nobly refused even to consider, only apparently they needed my help badly enough to resort to extreme measures…

Beth was silent for a while after I'd finished. I could tell she was deeply shocked by this glimpse into my fictitious, criminal past. She hadn't thought I was that kind of a guy.

"Of course," she said slowly, "I always knew there was *something*... You were never quite frank about... I thought it was just what you'd seen some terrible things over there and didn't want to talk about them."

She might look like an innocent college girl, but there were times when she was practically clairvoyant. It was very hard to keep up the act in the face of her steady regard. I forced myself to make a clumsy, embarrassed gesture, like a man who's got everything off his chest.

"Well," I said, "that's the story, Beth."

"And this woman," she said, "this woman who called you Eric...?"

I said, "We had code names for each other. But that's not what you're asking. The answer is yes."

After a moment, she asked, "What are you... What will you do?"

"Get Betsy back," I said. "Don't ask me how. You wouldn't want to know."

29

It was a dreary-looking place, mostly a great dusty parking lot with big trucks standing around—tankers, vans, and refrigerator jobs with compressors going, setting up a constant racket, like outboard motors. There was a big sign saying: TRUCKERS DISCOUNTS. The restaurant—cafe, we usually call it in this part of the world—wasn't as bad as it might have been, and there were some surprisingly shiny and expensive-looking cars with out-of-state license plates parked alongside. Somebody once told somebody that the place where the truckers stop is the place to eat, and tourists have been acting on that advice ever since. There may even be something to it.

In back, like poor relations, stood a bunch of little red-and-white clapboard shacks, relics of the days when a tourist cabin was a cabin, not a disembodied hotel room with TV, air-conditioning, and wall-to-wall carpeting. I stuck the Plymouth between an Arizona Chrysler and a California Volkswagen with a little sign on the back: DON'T SQUASH ME—I EAT HARMFUL INSECTS. It reminded me, for some reason, of the little blue Morris I'd encountered in Texas, also with a sign on the back; and I wondered what Mac had Shorty doing these days. I hoped it was something easy, after the rough time I'd given her in San Antonio.

But it was no time to be thinking of the women I'd known except one, and I took the paper-wrapped parcel from the seat beside me, got out of the car, walked along the line of cabins and, reaching the last one, knocked on the door.

Tina opened it. We looked at each other for a moment. She was wearing something that looked like a feminized bull-fighting costume, with a ruffled white shirt and tight white, embroidered pants ending approximately at the calves of her legs. I was glad she wasn't wearing a pretty dress. As I've mentioned before, my trousers-resistance is very high. She was making it easy for me.

"Come in, *chéri*," she said. "You are right on time. Your wife said you might be late."

I went past her into the gloom of the cabin. "I pushed right along," I said, turning to face her as she closed the door behind me. "Kind of a dump," I said, indicating the room.

She moved her shoulders. "One lives where one must. I have spent more time in worse places." She looked up at me and smiled. "What, Eric, no recriminations? Will you not tell me I'm an evil woman?"

"You're a bitch," I said, "but I knew that fifteen years

ago. I just made the mistake of forgetting it temporarily."

"I hated to deceive you," she said. "Really I did, *Liebchen.* I hated to trick you."

"Cut it out," I said. "You loved it. Every bit of it, playing me like a fish on a light leader, getting me to bury your dead and help your getaway, pretending to call up Mac for further instructions, heading me off with a lot of talk about security whenever I started getting nosy... Oh, it was a beautiful snow job, *querida,* and you enjoyed every minute of it. And you're enjoying this, too, aren't you? Bringing my family into the act—you resent them like hell, don't you, Tina?—and wondering just how I'm explaining all this to my wife."

She smiled. "You make me sound like a terrible person. But it is quite true, of course. I hate them. I hate her. She took you away from me. If it hadn't been for her, you would have come back to find me after the war. We would have been together, and maybe I would never... never have become what I am today."

I said, "A man who questioned me in San Antonio thought the card you showed me was your own."

"He was right," she said. "It is my card, and I am proud of it. There are very few of us who have earned that card. But it does not mean that I would not rather have done something else with my life. But you did not come. And I had to do something."

I asked, "Why did you change sides, Tina?"

"You ask that? Can you think of no reason why I should turn against America and everything American?" She laughed quickly. "No, *chéri*, I am not a silly, sentimental fool. I do not make the whole world pay for my broken heart. The fact is, I had certain talents, and when there was no longer a war to fight, I sold those talents to the highest bidder, as did many others of your wartime comrades. Ask Mac, he will tell you." She smiled. "I am very good, Eric. I command a very high price these days."

I nodded. "I got that impression." I patted the package under my arm. "This would be part of your price, no doubt."

"What is it?"

"Something you left behind in San Antonio. Nobody seemed to want it, so I brought it along."

"My furs?" She looked pleased. "That was sweet of you. I missed them very much. Put them on the bed... But we are wasting time. You are prepared to cooperate?"

"How?"

She raised her eyebrows. "Is it important? Did you ever ask Mac that question?"

"The circumstances were slightly different."

"Yes," she said. "Then it was only your life that was at stake."

I looked at her for a moment, and said, "Okay. You've made your point. Shoot."

She said, "You yield a little too easily, Eric. Could it be that you hope to be clever in spite of the warning I left at your house?" She waited. I didn't say anything. She said, "You have been followed ever since you left home. We are being watched right now, from a discreet distance. If anything at all should go wrong here, or if I should give a certain signal, the person watching us will go directly to where your little girl is being kept. He has his instructions, and he is not at all sentimental about children. Do you understand?"

I said, "It's clear. Who do I kill?"

She glanced at me quickly. "Do not say that as a joke, my dear. Would I require you for anything else *but* to kill?" After a moment, she said, "You know the target. I told you his name days ago. Everything I said then was the truth. I merely rearranged the cast of characters slightly." When I didn't speak, she went on: "It was always my intention to use you here in Santa Fe—under the pretense of working for Mac, of course. I was going to be very clever, so that you did not suspect our real purpose until too late.

But that girl intervened and delayed the execution of our plan. In a way this is much nicer. Now I can be frank. We want Amos Darrel dead. You will kill him for us."

There was silence in the little cabin, except for the chattering noise of a compressor unit on a truck parked outside. I looked at Tina thoughtfully, considering her proposition. You'll say it was a ridiculous idea. You'll say no sane person would expect another sane person to go out and kill somebody in cold blood, not even to save a child's life. But then, you didn't fight the war as we did. She was asking nothing really unreasonable, since she was asking it of me. We knew each other very well. I knew she'd do anything to Betsy she considered necessary. And she

knew I'd do anything for Betsy I considered necessary—
and if I had to do it to Amos, it was just tough on Amos.
He wasn't that good a friend of mine.

I asked, "Why me, Tina? You've got experts in your
outfit, I'm sure. You're pretty damn expert yourself, as I
recall. Why complicate it by dragging strangers off the
street to do your dirty work?"

She smiled. "My outfit, as you call it, must not be
known to exist. Because of the political repercussions.
That is why we prefer to work through local people, when
suitable ones are available. Besides, usually they know
the ground better. That is particularly true in your case,
since you're well acquainted with Dr. Darrel."

I said, deliberately naive, "But I have my home here!
You can't just ask me to go out and commit murder!"

She laughed. "*Chéri*, don't be childish. What is your
home to me? Nothing. Less than nothing. It is your
problem. If you can do it without being suspected, that
will be quite satisfactory to us. If you can't, you will stand
trial and go to prison. And you will tell a story of jealousy
or hatred or greed, or blind irresistible anger, anything to
satisfy the stupid authorities. Because you will know that
your wife and children are still vulnerable, and that if you
breathe a word of the truth, there will be a knife in the
night, or a bullet, a club, or a runaway car… You should
not have married, Eric. It puts you at the mercy of ruthless
people, people like me."

I said, "That's what you're really after, isn't it, Tina?"

"What do you mean?"

"You're getting your revenge, aren't you? After all these years. It's quite a production. First you take me from my wife, to show you still have the power to do it; and then you turn around and use my children to ruin me. You don't really care whether Amos Darrel lives or dies, not you! After the way this job's gone sour, the people you work for would probably prefer to have you pass it up now, rather than call further attention to their murderous activities. But you can't give it up, because you can't bear to think of me going back to my family and forgetting about you for the second time. I stood you up once, after the war, and I've got to pay for it."

She was silent for a little; then she sighed. "There is a lot of truth in what you say, but I do not think you're being quite fair."

I said, "Perhaps not. It doesn't really matter, does it?"

"No," she said. "Not now… You know Dr. Darrel quite well, of course, but I have here some data on his habits that may be useful to you. It's up to you, of course, but I'd like to point out that he drives the Los Alamos road every morning and evening. We could supply you with a heavy, fast car. It is a steep and winding road…"

I laughed. "Yes, sweetheart, and just how the hell am I going to catch Amos' souped-up Porsche on a steep and winding road in a heavy car? He could outrun a Jag on that hill. And even if I could run him off into the canyon, that little heap is built like a bank vault and he wears a safety belt; he'd bounce like a rubber ball and come up grinning… That's no good."

She said, "You see? That's why I picked you, because you know these things, not just for revenge. Well, choose your own method. I was just hoping you could make it look like an accident, for your sake... Eric?"

"Yes?"

"I asked you once not to hate me. Don't you see? We all do what we have to do. There is no choice."

"No," I said. "No choice at all."

Then I hit her.

30

Mac used to have a little lecture he gave when he was putting the final polish on us.

"Dignity," he'd say. "Remember that dignity is the key to any man's resistance, or any woman's. As long as your subject is allowed to feel that he's still a human being with rights and privileges and self-respect, he can usually hold out indefinitely. Take, for instance, a soldier in a clean uniform, lead him politely to a desk, seat him decorously on a chair, request him to place his hands before him, stick splinters under his fingernails, and set fire to them… and you'll be surprised how often he'll watch his fingertips cooking and laugh in your face. But if you take the same man, first, and work him over to show that you don't mind bruising your knuckles and don't have a bit of respect for his integrity as a man—you don't have to hurt him much, just mess him up until he can no longer cling to a romanticized picture of himself as a noble and handsome embodiment of stubborn courage…"

* * *

I'd caught her completely by surprise. She went back
against the wall with a crash that shook the cabin; then
she slid to the floor, her legs gracelessly apart, her eyes
wide and stunned. Slowly, looking up at me in shocked
wonder, she put her hand to her mouth, took it away, and
looked at the blood on the palm. Outside, the compressor
kept up its outboard-motor clatter.

Tina shook her head to clear it, and pushed her hand
along her thigh to wipe it clean, leaving an ugly smear on
the white trousers. She started to push herself to her feet. I
reached down and hauled her up by the front of her fancy
shirt, feeling buttons, cloth, and stitching give way under
the strain. Holding her by the bunched material, I slapped
her repeatedly until her short, dark hair was whipping
across her face and her nose was bleeding. Then I shoved
her away from me hard. She stumbled backwards, turned,
tried to catch herself, and went heavily to hands and
knees. It was too good an opportunity to miss. I put my
foot in her rear and pushed, so that she pitched forward
and slid a couple of feet across the dusty wooden floor on
her face and stomach. Since we were evening old scores,
I might as well collect for the time I'd got the short end of
that horseplay in the desert.

I waited for her to pick herself up and pull herself
together. I had shut off my mind completely. There was
nothing to think about—except what I had to do.

Waiting, I said, "If you come up with a weapon,

darling, I'll kick your face in."

It was a different Tina who climbed slowly to her feet and turned to face me: a torn, dirty, and bloody creature— oddly sexless, thank God—that wiped its mouth and nose on the rags of its shirt and cleaned its hands on the seat of its pants without a downward glance at the damage that had been inflicted upon it. Not a pretty woman who'd been hurt, with some instinctive concern for her appearance, but a wary, wounded animal at bay, with eyes only for the hunter.

"You fool!" she breathed. "What do you think to gain?" She had taken a step sideways; suddenly she was at the window. The blind flew up with a clatter. She wheeled to face me again. Her expression was savage. "There! Loris will go now! I warned you. Now it is too late. No matter what you do to me, it is too late!"

I grinned at her, and picked up the paper-wrapped package from the bed, and tossed it at her. She wasn't prepared for the weight of it. She caught it all right, but it pushed her back a step.

"Open it," I said.

She glanced at me. I saw her eyes widen slightly with speculation, perhaps with a hint of fear. She came forward to the bed, set the package down, and ripped off the paper, revealing nothing but mink and satin lining. She glanced at me again, and started to unfold the stole carefully, and stopped, staring at what it contained. I heard her breath catch at the sight of Loris's big revolver lying there. Around it, the glossy fur was matted with the half-dried blood that had been on the weapon. It looked like something ugly and dangerous that had fouled its nest.

"You would send warnings to my wife," I murmured. "Tina, you're a fool. I didn't get to be Mac's best boy by trembling at dead cats."

She recognized the gun of course. After a moment, she reached out and touched it, quite gently. "He is dead?"

"Probably, by this time," I said. "He'd have needed a new heart and lungs to keep on living. You're through, Tina."

She swung about to look at me. She hadn't really heard me. She was still thinking about Loris. I don't suppose she'd loved the man, and certainly, from what I'd seen this morning, he'd felt no need to be faithful to her. I think it must have been for her something like losing an arm—a strong and useful appendage, unable to think for itself of course, but how much do you expect of an arm, anyway? They'd made a good team, I suspected, better than she and I; we'd had too many brains and ambitions between us.

She said softly, "He was a better man than you, Eric."

"Probably," I said. "In the strict sense of the word. But I wasn't competing with him in the matter of masculinity. He may have been a better man, but he wasn't much of a killer."

"If he'd got his hands on you…"

"If that bed had wings we could fly it," I said. "When did I ever let a big hunk of beef like that get its hands on me? Well, once, granted, when I wasn't expecting trouble.

But I'm back in the old groove now, darling. You've put me right back into it. And I never saw a muscle boy yet who worried me, certainly not this one, with ivory between the ears." I looked at her standing before me in her wrecked shirt and her silly white pants, soiled and split at the knees. She looked very much like a kid that had got into a scrap and got its nose bloodied... I put the thought aside. It was no time for drawing sentimental valentines. She was no kid. She was a dangerous woman, responsible for many deaths and at least one kidnaping. I said it again: "Tina you're through. Mac sends his greetings."

She gave me again that little speculative, half-fearful widening of the eyes. "He sent *you*?"

I said, "You can have it hard or easy. Don't kid yourself for a moment, Tina. Look in the mirror. I didn't muss you up for fun; I just wanted to show you I'm quite prepared to get my hands dirty. We can save both of us a lot of trouble if you'll just take my word that I can be just as tough as I have to."

She said quickly, "Your child. Your little girl. If I don't send word by a certain time..."

"What time?" I said. "This won't take very long."

"You're bluffing!" she cried. "You don't dare."

"With Loris loose I wouldn't," I said. "Which is why I removed him. Don't talk dare to me, Tina. I don't know what instructions you left with the people who are holding Betsy, but hurting a baby, a baby who can't even talk, who can't be a witness against you, takes a strong stomach. Maybe they can do it and maybe they can't, but it'll take them a while to work up to it without direct orders. And who's going to give those orders? Not Loris. Not you."

She whispered, "You can't!"

I laughed. "This is your old friend Eric, sweetheart. You made a mistake. Mac asked me to go after you, did you know that? We had a long talk in San Antonio, Mac and I. I told him to go to hell. I told him I was out of it, I wasn't mad at anybody, I was a peaceful citizen with a home and family, and I wasn't going back to them with anybody's blood on my hands. I'd spent a dozen years washing it off, I said, and I didn't want to get the smell back again... That's what I told him. And I made it stick. There was also a small matter of sentiment, perhaps. And then you sent Loris to snatch my child!" I drew a long breath. "You never had any kids, Tina? If you had, you'd never have touched a hair of one of mine." There was silence in the room, but outside the compressor kept chattering away. I said quietly, "Now you'd better tell me where she is."

She licked her lips. "Better men than you have tried to make me talk, Eric."

I said, "This doesn't take better men, sweetheart. This takes worse men. And at the moment, with my kid in danger, I'm just about as bad as they come."

I took a step forward. She took a step backwards; then, abruptly, she ducked towards the bed and came up with Loris' big revolver in her hand. I don't suppose she really expected it to work, but there was a chance and she had to take it. She didn't hesitate, she didn't warn or threaten me, she just aimed it at me point-blank and pulled the trigger. I laughed in her face as the hammer fell on an empty chamber. I'd have deserved to die if I'd been fool enough to leave the thing loaded.

I ducked as she hurled it at my head. Then she put a hand inside her torn shirt, and I heard the whisper of steel as the blade of the parachutist's knife slid out and locked, but she'd never been much good with edged weapons. I took the knife away from her in less than ten seconds. This wasn't a game, like that time in the desert; I wasn't holding back any, and something snapped. She gave a little cry and fell back against the wall, hugging her broken wrist. She watched me approach. Her eyes were black with hate.

"You'll never find her!" she hissed. "I'll never tell you, even if you kill me!"

I glanced at the knife in my hand, and tested the point with my thumb. Her eyes widened slightly.

"You'll tell," I said.

31

I dried my hands and came out of the bathroom. A small sound made me swing around sharply to look towards the window. Beth was there.

I stared at her blankly for a moment. She was straddling the sill awkwardly. She must have tried the door and found it locked, and had gone around to the side and got the sash up while I had the water running and couldn't hear her. Apparently she'd started to climb inside and had got this far when she'd seen Tina, lying by the opposite wall. Now she was just sitting there, half in and half out. Her face was absolutely white and her eyes were enormous.

I walked over and pulled her inside. Then I closed the window and drew the blind. Leaving her standing there, I crossed the room and picked up the Colt Woodsman I'd laid aside after using it. I took the clip out and wiped it carefully. I replaced the clip and wiped off the gun. I fitted Tina's hand around the butt and let the gun fall naturally to the floor nearby. Then I got to my feet and stood looking down for a moment, after which I checked the room with my eyes. Besides the gun, which I had to leave, there wasn't anything there that belonged to me, except my wife.

I went over and automatically put my hand on her arm to guide her to the door, but she drew quickly away. Well, that figured. I went outside without touching her again. She followed me. Her station wagon was parked in front. I hoped nobody'd seen it who had a good memory. I'd completed my part of the deal, and Mac would cover up for me, but I didn't want to make it too hard for him. Of course, once the police checked the gun and found that it had killed not only Tina and Loris but Barbara Herrera as well, they'd be able to make a nice triangle story of it—the madly jealous wife killing her younger rival, getting carved up by her husband when he learned of her crime, shooting him five times in return, and, after he'd staggered off to die, turning the gun on herself. Any small discrepancies would get lost in the shuffle, under Mac's careful supervision.

I walked around to the driver's seat while Beth got in on the near side. As usual, after she'd been driving the car, I had to run the seat back to make room for my legs. I drove out of there, and stopped at a shopping center a mile up the road.

I asked, "What the hell brought you out there, anyway?"

Her voice was a whisper: "I… I just couldn't wait at home…"

I said, "I told you that you wouldn't want to know how I went about it." She glanced at me, and licked her lips, but didn't speak. I took a pencil and a piece of paper from the glove compartment, wrote down a phone number, drew a line, and wrote an address below it. I gave her the paper and put the pencil back. I said, "I'm not exactly in condition to make a public appearance at the moment, and we can save a little time if you'll go into that drugstore and make a call. Have you got a dime? Call the number I've written there. Ask for Mr. Calhoun. Tell him that Betsy's at the address below. It's a little lane in one of those adobe rabbit warrens down along Agua Fria Street, I think. Tell them they'd better get help from some local cops who speak Spanish and know the area."

Beth hesitated. "Can we... can we go there?"

I said, "No, it's a job for experts; leave them to it. But I think it's going to be all right."

She said, "Matt, I—" She started to reach out and touch my arm, but she couldn't quite make herself do it. She was still seeing the locked room and the thing on the floor. She'd always see that, now, when she looked at me.

She took her hand back, and opened the car door, and got out. I watched her run into the drugstore, clutching the piece of paper; and I wondered how soon Mac would get in touch with me again. I didn't think he'd wait very long. Reliable help is hard to get these days. I didn't think it would be too long before he'd have another job for a good man in that line of business.

I sat there and wondered how I'd answer him, when he came. The terrible thing was, I didn't really know…

ABOUT THE AUTHOR

Donald Hamilton was the creator of secret agent Matt Helm, star of 27 novels that have sold more than 20 million copies worldwide.

Born in Sweden, he emigrated to the United States and studied at the University of Chicago. During the Second World War he served in the United States Naval Reserve, and in 1941 he married Kathleen Stick, with whom he had four children.

The first Matt Helm book, *Death of a Citizen*, was published in 1960 to great acclaim, and four of the subsequent novels were made into motion pictures. Hamilton was also the author of several outstanding stand-alone thrillers and westerns, including two novels adapted for the big screen as *The Big Country* and *The Violent Men*.

Donald Hamilton died in 2006.

COMING SOON FROM TITAN BOOKS

The Matt Helm Series
BY DONALD HAMILTON

The long-awaited return of the United States'
toughest special agent.

The Wrecking Crew
The Removers (April 2013)
The Silencers (June 2013)
Murderers' Row (August 2013)
The Ambushers (October 2013)
The Shadowers (December 2013)
The Ravagers (February 2014)

COMING SOON FROM TITAN BOOKS

PRAISE FOR DONALD HAMILTON

"Donald Hamilton has brought to the spy novel
the authentic hard realism of Dashiell Hammett;
and his stories are as compelling, and probably
as close to the sordid truth of espionage,
as any now being told."
Anthony Boucher, *The New York Times*

"This series by Donald Hamilton is the top-ranking
American secret agent fare, with its intelligent
protagonist and an author who consistently writes
in high style. Good writing, slick plotting and
stimulating characters, all tartly flavored with wit."
Book Week

"Matt Helm is as credible a man of violence as has
ever figured in the fiction of intrigue."
The New York Sunday Times

"Fast, tightly written, brutal, and very good…"
Milwaukee Journal

TITANBOOKS.COM

The Man From Hell
by Barrie Roberts

Séance For A Vampire
by Fred Saberhagen

The Seventh Bullet
by Daniel D. Victor

The Whitechapel Horrors
by Edward B. Hanna

Dr. Jekyll and Mr. Holmes
by Loren D. Estleman

The Angel of the Opera
by Sam Siciliano

The Giant Rat of Sumatra
by Richard L. Boyer

The Peerless Peer
by Philip José Farmer

The Star of India
by Carole Buggé

TITANBOOKS.COM